THE HAUNTING OF DUNGEON CREEK

Phil Roxbee Cox

Illustrated by
Jane Gedye

Series Editor: Gaby Waters
Assistant Editor: Michelle Bates

Contents

Reader Beware . . .

This is a chilling ghost story – but there's more to it than meets the eye. The mystery will unravel as the story unfolds, but if you keep your eyes open you may be able to stay one step ahead of the action.

Vital information might be lurking anywhere. On almost every double page there are things that could help you. The pictures are important, so look at them carefully. But don't be fooled. There may be some false clues . . .

Page 48 will give you some hints of what to look for. You can refer to this page as you go along or look at it at the end to see if you missed anything.

In the Beginning

What later became a strange and terrifying adventure for brothers Boz and JJ started simply enough with a stroll around a local market. The weather was sunny, and the place was the fishing village of Dungeon Creek.

"Wow!" said Boz, picking up an old pistol. "This would be a great present to buy Mr. Barkis as a thank you for letting us stay with him. Then he saw how much it cost. "Err, perhaps not," he added, hurriedly putting it down.

They spent another hour at the market, which sold everything from fish to furniture. This was much more fun than shopping at home. If JJ hadn't tripped and landed flat on his face, they might have avoided all the trouble that lay ahead – unless, of course, other strange forces were at work that day. But JJ did trip and, as he picked himself up and put his glasses back on, something caught his eye. A glint of gold winked at him from under a blanket.

JJ pulled back the blanket. The gold was an ornately carved wooden picture frame. Boz stepped back to study his brother's find. It was an oil painting, dark with age. "We must buy this painting, JJ," he said strangely. "We must own it. The painting has to be ours."

A Mysterious Message

Boz and JJ took the painting straight back to the cottage where they were staying with their parents' friend, Mr. Barkis. This place was so old that the timbers were all crooked and the floors weren't even level. There weren't any cottages like that back in their home town.

"Look what we've just bought," said JJ, plonking the painting down in front of Mr. Barkis, who was reading a spooky book about a ghost train.

Their host picked up the picture. "You bought this at the market?" he asked, studying their purchase carefully. "It must be at least two hundred years old, you know. How much did it cost you?" When they told him, he was impressed. "It must be worth more than that," he said. JJ and Boz knew that Mr. Barkis must have some idea what he was talking about. He made his living making and selling copies of antique furniture.

Mr. Barkis put down the painting and left the room. He went out to his workshop and crashed around for a while. He returned with a triumphant look on his face and a bottle and a cloth in his hands.

What's that for, Mr. Barkis?

You'll see.

He poured some liquid from the bottle onto the cloth, then gently began to rub the painting with it. The result was dramatic. Centuries of grime were wiped away in an instant. What had been dull areas of brown now revealed their original glow. Bold brushstrokes were shown off in all their glory.

"I thought the dark shape at the front was supposed to be a rock," Boz pointed. "But it's a woman . . . and the sea really looks as if it's moving. In fact, it makes me feel queasy just looking at it."

SI RE VERA ME REQUIRIS DIC NOMEN MEUM TUM TIBI ADSTABO

"And what have we here?" said Mr. Barkis, with a final rub of the cloth. "It's writing." He leaned forward and peered at it, his nose almost touching the canvas. "Hmm. How very strange. How very interesting."

"They don't look like any words I've ever seen before," said JJ, trying to see past Mr. Barkis's head. His glasses were steaming up in the heat of the room.

"That's because they're written in Latin," said Barkis.

"What do they mean?" asked Boz. He ran his fingertips across the painted letters. They felt icy cold. He shuddered. His mind was filled with a strange sense of urgency. "We have to find out what they mean . . . "

5

Stranger in the Night

That night, only their third in Dungeon Creek, JJ and Boz were awoken by a loud CRASH from downstairs. "What was that?" said JJ sitting bolt upright. He banged his head on the bottom of Boz's bunk above him.

"It sounded like breaking glass," said Boz, sitting up with a start. He banged his head on the ceiling. "Ouch! Perhaps Mr. Barkis just stretched and put his elbow through the window," he grinned. "This cottage isn't very big."

"It's three o'clock in the morning. Even *he* must be in bed by now," said JJ, lowering his voice to a whisper. "Let's go downstairs and investigate. It could just be a cat."

Cautiously, they crept out of their bedroom, across the sloping landing to the bannisters. They then edged their way down the rickety old stairs – step by creaking step – sometimes stopping for fear of being heard. Their hearts began to beat faster as they tiptoed into the moonlit room. This was no cat. The boys had walked in on a burglary. In the moonlight streaming through a broken window, they could make out the shadowy form of *someone about to make off with their painting!*

Boz wished that he was carrying the old pistol they'd seen at the market. JJ wished that he was three feet taller and didn't wear glasses. Neither of them was sure of the best way to tackle a real live burglar caught in the act, but they had to do something.

6

JJ mouthed the words "What shall we do?" without making a sound, but his brother understood him.

"Stay right where you are!" Boz called out, in the deepest voice he could muster. The intruder did the exact opposite, dropping the painting and scrambling out of the window. The brothers rushed over to the window. They glimpsed the outline retreating before it disappeared into the night. Both were sure that they had seen the silhouetted figure somewhere before.

A few moments later, the front door flew open and a light went on. Barkis stepped into the room carrying a pile of firewood. "What on earth are you two doing up at this time of night?" he asked with a puzzled frown.

What's going on?

"We've just chased off a burglar who was trying to steal our painting," explained JJ. "He got away through the window."

"Really?" said Mr. Barkis. "The thieving swine must have waited for me to slip out to my workshop before sneaking in. Good work, boys." He didn't sound particularly concerned. Boz suggested they call the police. Mr. Barkis dropped a log on his own foot. "That won't be necessary," he said quickly. "The only harm done is a broken window, and that's easily fixed in the morning. Back to bed the pair of you." So back to bed they went. But Boz and JJ didn't sleep a wink.

7

A Voice from the Past

When Boz and JJ went downstairs the next morning, Mr. Barkis had already made their breakfast and was busy mending the broken window. Boz's eyes fixed on the painting. The image of the woman staring out of the canvas had filled his thoughts throughout his sleepless night. It was almost as if she had been trying to call out to him.

"Interested in the Latin inscription on your painting?" asked Mr. Barkis, interrupting his thoughts. Boz nodded, his mouth full of toast. "Then you should go and see Mr. Tigg at the schoolhouse. Latin used to be taught in most schools a long time ago, and Mr. Tigg became a teacher a very long time ago indeed." He closed the window, chuckling to himself.

"Let's copy down the inscription rather than lug a valuable two-hundred-year-old oil painting around Dungeon Creek with us," JJ suggested. Boz had to admit it was a good idea.

"I don't want to dampen your excitement," said Mr. Barkis. "But I didn't say your picture was *valuable*. I simply said that it's worth more than you paid for it. I wouldn't start planning any exotic trips abroad just yet if I were you." He closed the window and put the lid on his tin of putty.

"Somebody thought it was worth stealing," JJ reminded him. "I'm not sure what else they would want from here." Mr. Barkis glared at the boy. "Er, no disrespect, Mr. Barkis," JJ added hurridly.

JJ and Boz found Mr. Tigg at the schoolhouse. He was outside raking up leaves. JJ explained who they were, and asked if he would mind translating some Latin for them.

Without a word, the old man dropped his rake and marched into the schoolhouse. Boz and JJ were beginning to wonder whether they'd said something to upset him, when he returned wearing a pair of glasses.

"Can't read a thing without them," he said. JJ handed him the piece of paper with the words copied onto it. "Hmm. It's straightforward enough," said the old teacher.

> SI RE VERA ME
> REQUIRIS DIC
> NOMEN MEUM
> TUM TIBI ADSTABO

"We thought *vera* might be a woman's name," said Boz. "And *tibi* a cat's, but we were stuck after that."

"No, no, no," groaned Mr Tigg. "What your mysterious inscription says is, '*if you truly need me, say my name and I shall be there to aid you*'."

Boz repeated the words. "*If you truly need me, say my name and I shall be there to aid you*. What a strange message. I wonder who it was meant for? '*Say my name*' must mean the name of the woman. She's the only person in the painting." He had to find out her name. He just *had* to. Meanwhile, a pair of unblinking eyes watched the three of them from nearby.

9

The Name in the Frame

Back at the cottage, Mr. Barkis peered at the canvas through a special kind of magnifying glass. He held it up to his eye and bent over the painting. Boz was convinced that the woman's name must be written somewhere on the canvas. Mr. Barkis handed the eyeglass to Boz.

"Her name must be hidden somewhere in the picture," said Boz. "It probably won't be too obvious. After all, it's tied up with that cryptic Latin message. Finding her name should help us make sense of what it all means."

JJ agreed. "I expect whoever painted this didn't want her name to be too easy to find," said JJ. "After all, the message telling us to find her name was written in Latin to make it difficult to understand."

Barkis sat down in his chair and picked up his book about the ghost train. "When that message was written, plenty of people would have understood Latin," he pointed out. "And isn't it '*say* my name' not '*find* my name'?"

Boz said nothing, then his brother whooped with delight. "Look," said JJ. "I've found a name . . . but it doesn't sound like a woman's." He pointed.

"That must be the name of the painter," Boz sighed. His face fell.

"It's a good start though," said Mr. Barkis. "The name Guppy sounds familiar. Why not go down to the library and look it up there?"

10

Boz and JJ put their jackets back on and left the cottage for the second time that day. As they walked down the overgrown path to the gate, they saw Mr. Barkis disappear into his workshop.

"I like Mr. Barkis," said JJ. "But there is something a little mysterious about him. Don't you think so?"

His elder brother shrugged. "It's the painting I find mysterious," he said. The image of the woman on the rocks flashed through his mind.

The two boys began walking down the country lane which led to the village. At that moment, there was the ring of a bell, and an elderly woman on an even older bicycle whizzed past them at great speed.

"That was the lady who sold us the painting!" cried Boz. "Perhaps she can tell us more about it."

They called after the woman but either she didn't hear them, or she chose to ignore their calls. Boz and JJ chased after her but, moments later, she had disappeared around a bend.

"Perhaps she thinks we're a pair of dissatisfied customers who want our money back," JJ grinned. Bending forward to catch his breath, he rested his arm on a gate at the side of the road. His brother's eyes widened in amazement. "What is it?" JJ demanded.

Boz pointed to two small words on a letter box.

SILAS GUPPY

To the Lighthouse

Intrigued, Boz and JJ pushed open the gate and began to follow a very long and winding path. It led them through coarse grass, past thorny bushes, in the direction of the sea.

"This is weird," said JJ. "It's like a case of *déjà vu*."

"Isn't that the place in France where crazy Cousin Colin lives?" asked Boz. JJ groaned. He couldn't tell whether his brother was joking or not.

"It's a feeling that you've been somewhere before, even though it's really the first time you've been there," JJ explained. "I feel that now."

"That's exactly how I'm feeling too," said Boz excitedly. Their surroundings were strangely familiar. It was almost as if they were experiencing someone else's memory of the place. For the umpteenth time, the image of the woman in the painting flashed through Boz's mind.

Suddenly, the sun disappeared behind a cloud, and the gloomy light made the sea seem strangely different. The waves looked like the vivid brushstrokes of oil paint. No wonder. This was the very stretch of coastline in the picture!

The path took them down to the shore, and ended right in front of a stretch of rocks leading all the way out to an offshore lighthouse. The lighthouse rose majestically into the cloud-filled sky.

All feelings of uneasiness were forgotten in an instant. "This is fantastic," said JJ. Together they set off across the rocks, the seawater lapping at their ankles.

The boys reached the lighthouse to find the door slightly open. "I never thought I'd get to go inside a real lighthouse," said Boz. "Come on!"

"Shouldn't we knock, or something?" suggested JJ, a little nervously. "If the door's open it probably means that someone's at home."

"If they are, they'll never hear us down here," replied Boz. "We'll shout out on the way up."

The boys went inside and began climbing the cold dark stairs. The place smelled musty with age and dank with salt water. JJ began to feel breathless, and it wasn't just the climb. The air was getting more and more stale with every step.

They paused to catch their breath. Then, just as they were about to set off again, they heard a strange flapping noise up ahead in the echoing gloom. Nervously, Boz stepped forward. Beating wings flapped around him, fanning air against his cheek. He cried out in terror.

13

The Many Faces of Silas Guppy

Boz and JJ laughed with relief when they realized what the creature was. This was no huge and terrifying bat but only a cheeky myna bird.

"Hullo boys! Hullo boys!" cried the bird, circling above their heads as they made their way up to an open door. The brothers wondered if there were any other occupants inside the lighthouse.

Boz knocked. "Is there anybody there?" he called out, just in case a lighthouse keeper was lurking in the shadows. They still felt a bit shaken by the bat that wasn't a bat. The silence was broken by another squawk from the bird. Boz pushed the door open wide.

They found themselves in a large round room. What struck JJ and Boz was the furniture. It must have been specially made for the lighthouse. The lighthouse walls were curved, and so was the back of the furniture. It all fitted perfectly, but would look very out of place in an ordinary house.

14

Boz's eyes were drawn to the pictures hanging on the far side of the room. Some were drawings, some were paintings, and some were photographs. Each was a picture of a man and under each and every one of them was a different date, but the same name. The name was Silas Guppy. In an instant, Boz was reminded of what had first led them down the path and to this place. He had forgotten in all the excitement.

JJ came over and stood by his brother. He gasped. They studied the pictures together in silence. Surely they were all of the same man? Okay, so his hair was different in each picture, but his features were the same. "This is crazy" JJ protested. "The earliest picture is dated two hundred years ago, but some of them are only a few years old!"

"And, if Guppy painted our picture of the woman with the mysterious Latin message on it, what's he doing smiling at us out of a photo dated nineteen ninety?" Boz gulped. "I'm beginning to think there's something weird about Dungeon Creek and not just the painting." At that moment, the curved door behind them slammed shut, as if pulled by some invisible hand. It left the brothers with a loud THUD ringing in their ears.

15

Trapped!

The door wouldn't budge. JJ and Boz pushed it and pulled it. JJ even punched it, but that was more in frustration than thinking it would do any good. The door stayed firmly shut.

"Perhaps there's another way out of here," Boz suggested.

"I don't see how," sighed JJ. "The stairs ended on the other side of the door and that ladder over there must lead up to where the light is."

Do you think it was the wind?

Sure. What else could have slammed it shut?

"Then we'll have to try to lever the door open. Let's see if we can find something to slip between it and the frame," said Boz. JJ and Boz searched the room from top to bottom. They couldn't find anything to use as a lever.

Boz sat on the floor in the middle of the room and rested his chin in his hands. "Perhaps we're going about this the wrong way," he suggested. "If we can't open the door, maybe we should leave by the window."

JJ opened the small metal-framed window and looked down to the rocks below. They seemed a long way off and made him feel dizzy. "We'd need a very long rope to reach the ground from here" he sighed.

He slammed the window shut and joined Boz on the floor. They would just have to wait for Guppy, or whoever the lighthouse keeper was, to return from wherever he was . . .

They both spotted the chest at about the same time. A corner of it was sticking out from under the metal-framed bed. The two boys leaped to their feet and dragged it out into the open. It looked like an old seaman's chest from a swashbuckling pirate story.

"There may be some rope in here," said JJ doubtfully. The lid wouldn't open. The hefty chest was locked.

16

Boz had spied a set of keys hanging on a hook by the stove, and hurried over to fetch them. After a few false starts, they found a key that fitted both of the locks perfectly. It was obvious that the old chest hadn't been opened for years. The locks creaked and squeaked in protest as the key released the rusty mechanisms.

Throwing back the lid, Boz and JJ were rewarded with the intriguing sight of ancient charts, old books, a ship-in-a-bottle, and curious hodge podge of items to do with sailing and the sea.

All thoughts of escaping were forgotten as the two brothers began studying the contents of the trunk. Boz picked up an old leather bound book and began to read. What he read was so vivid, so gripping, that it somehow came alive for him. He could almost see the events unfolding like a play . . .

A Tale of Treachery

This is incredible. Listen.

. . . The year is 1783. The place is Dungeon Creek.

1

At night, its treacherous rocks are lighted with lanterns to warn passing ships to steer clear.

I feel a storm brewing.

2

But a gang of local villains who call themselves 'wreckers' have other ideas. They snuff out the lanterns on the rocks . . .

3

. . . and light one of their own on the beach to trick the ships into coming too close inland . . .

Ooh, there'll be rich pickings tonight.

4

. . . so that they smash on to the rocks.

CRUNCH!

5

Escape and Failure

It was beginning to get dark as Boz and JJ sat in the circular room thinking about the evil wreckers of years gone by.

Now that there was a proper lighthouse in Dungeon Creek, there was no fear of any modern ships striking the rocks below.

Their thoughts were interrupted by a loud hum of electricity as the huge revolving light came to life in the lamp room above them. They looked up in amazement, startled by the noise.

"This lighthouse must be on an automatic time switch," said Boz.

"That means that there's no need to have a lighthouse keeper any more," sighed JJ. "I don't think anyone has slept in that bed for a very long time."

A mouse stared out at them from a hole in the mattress.

"*We* may have to sleep in it," Boz pointed out. "It could be days or even months before anyone finds us."

All this talk of beds gave Boz a flash of inspiration. He went over to the huge wardrobe that he had searched earlier, and took some faded sheets from inside one of the drawers.

"I don't know why I didn't think of this before!" he said excitedly. "I've had one of my great ideas." JJ looked more than a little doubtful.

20

The 'great idea' was to tie the sheets together to make a rope. It wasn't nearly long enough to reach all the way down to the ground. However, it was long enough for them to climb out of the window and in through the one below.

JJ went first. The brothers had tossed a coin to see who it would be, and JJ had lost. The vicious wind lashed against him as he clung to the rope. Once he almost lost his glasses, then his grip as he pushed them back up his nose. One slip and he could end up falling onto the rocks below.

He made it! Pushing the lower window open with his feet, he found himself back in the spiral stairwell. Boz soon followed him.

They hurried down the stairs and threw open the front door, only to find that the tide had risen. The rock path they'd crossed from the beach was now covered by crashing waves. They were trapped for the night after all.

Rescue from the Rocks

Out of the darkness a small boat appeared, rowed through the foaming waves by a girl with chestnut brown hair. With great skill, she brought the tiny wooden craft as close to Boz and JJ as she could. Just below the surface of the sea lurked the dangerous rocks that could rip the boat to shreds.

"Step into the water there," the girl pointed. "It's shallow, but be careful not to slip," she cried above the wind.

JJ and Boz did as she commanded, wading over to the boat and clambering into it. Immediately, the girl began rowing away into deeper, safer water. Every time the sweeping path of light from the revolving lighthouse lamp illuminated the boat, its three occupants took on an eerie glow.

"Thank you for saving us," said Boz. "JJ and I didn't fancy spending a cold night in a lighthouse." A seagull screeched with laughter somewhere in the sky. "You haven't told us your name."

"Katherine," she said, her eyes glinting in the twilight. "My name is Katherine. You must be careful of Dungeon Creek's treacherous tides."

It only took a few minutes for the boat to reach the shore. It was then that Boz and JJ were in for yet another surprise. When Katherine had beached the boat in a particular place on the sand, she used her arms to swing herself out of the boat and into an enormous old-fashioned wheelchair.

Katherine was aware of Boz and JJ's amazement. "What's the big deal?" she asked. "You're pretty acrobatic yourselves, swinging through the lighthouse window like that. It was the white sheets that caught my eye."

"It was lucky you spotted us," said JJ. They followed Katherine up a ramp designed for boats to slide down to the water, and found themselves on a flat path running between the cliffs.

Katherine asked what they'd been doing in the lighthouse. "Trying to find out more about a man named Silas Guppy," JJ told her with caution.

"There's been a Silas Guppy in Dungeon Creek for hundreds of years," said Katherine. "And the last six of them have all been lighthouse keepers."

"You mean there's more than one Silas Guppy?" asked Boz, feeling very foolish. Why hadn't he thought of such an obvious explanation?

A smile passed across Katherine's lips. "Of course," she said. "Every first son of a Silas Guppy was called Silas all the way down through the years. The very last Silas Guppy was the very last lighthouse keeper. He never had a son so, when he died, it was decided to control the lighthouse with electric machinery."

"Were all the Silas Guppys painters too?" asked JJ.

"Painters? I was wondering if that was why you went to the lighthouse," said Katherine, bringing her wheelchair to a halt. "I believe you have something of mine and I want it back." A strange expression crossed Katherine's face. For that one fleeting moment, she reminded Boz of another face – one that was beginning to haunt him. It was a face created from brushstrokes and oil paint by a man named Guppy. Katherine had looked exactly like the woman in the painting.

23

A Name at Last

Boz, JJ and Katherine made their way to Mr. Barkis's cottage in silence. Katherine hadn't been invited, but there was an unspoken understanding that she should go back with them. After all, she had rescued them hadn't she? And she knew about their painting, even claiming that it was hers.

Mr. Barkis didn't seem at all surprised or worried that they'd returned from a 'trip to the library' so late and so wet. They found him in his workshop. It was the first time the boys had been right inside. Their host was busy whipping a table using strips of rope studded with small nails.

"This makes a piece of wood look old," he quickly explained. "It's called distressing it. I'm doing two or three hundred years' worth of damage to this table in one evening. By the time I've finished with it, it will look like a genuine antique."

JJ introduced Katherine to Mr. Barkis. "Oh, I know Katherine and she knows me," he said. "How's your Aunt Lilian, Katherine?"

"As gloomy as ever," grinned Katherine. "I'm here about the oil painting, Mr. Barkis. My aunt had no right to sell it to JJ and Boz. It belongs to me."

"Oh, it's *that* painting is it? Well, that's for your aunt and you three to sort out between you," said Barkis. "Why not go inside and talk it over?"

24

When Katherine entered the cottage, she caught sight of the painting. The flickering glow of an old oil lamp cast a strange glow on the canvas. The painted waves appeared to be moving like the real thing. "You've cleaned it!" she cried. "You've uncovered *her*." Then Katherine spotted the Latin inscription. "What's this?" she asked, moving closer.

For reasons he couldn't explain, Boz was reluctant to tell Katherine anything just yet. Perhaps it was because he felt that she was hiding things from them.

"The ship in the background is supposed to be the very last ship smashed on the rocks in Dungeon Creek by the wreckers," she told them, with a shudder.

"Have you any idea who the woman in the painting is?" asked Boz. Katherine had obviously known about her, even though her image had been covered in centuries of grime.

"Oh yes," replied Katherine, her eyes avoiding theirs. "I know about *her*. Her name was Reckless Rose. She was leader of the Dungeon Creek wreckers." It was she who lured so many ships to the trecherous rock and so many unsuspecting sailors to their doom."

At last they knew the name of the woman whose face had been crowding Boz's mind since he first laid eyes on the painting "She was supposed to be a witch," said Katheine quietly. Boz and JJ looked at each other.

"Superstitious old garbage," said JJ, watching the waves on the canvas with a queasy feeling inside.

"That's as maybe," said Katherine. "But I am a direct descendant of Rose, and some people take that garbage very seriously indeed."

25

Katherine's Tale

For JJ it was simply exciting to learn more about the painting, and to meet someone related to a so-called witch. To Boz, Katherine's news was much more than that. Somehow Reckless Rose had been haunting his thoughts ever since the moment the painting had been cleaned. Now he knew her name.

"What happened to Reckless Rose?" asked JJ. He had heard about the treatment of so-called witches in history lessons.

"Now there's a story," said Katherine, and she began her strange tale, filling their minds with images of past deeds . . .

After years of rich picking from helpless drowning sailors . . .

Another successful night, Rose.

1

. . . Rose and her wreckers were finally caught by the army of 'Redcoats'.

2

She wasn't put on trial with the rest of her gang . . .

You shall pay for your evil crimes.

3

. . . but was declared to be a witch. Yes, the God-fearing people of Dungeon Creek still believed in witches.

Witch!

Devil woman!

4

Rose was dragged from her prison cell to be burned at the stake . . .

5

. . . But legend has it that the fire couldn't harm her. She stepped through the flames and walked away.

6

"What happened next?" asked JJ when Katherine had finished her story. If Rose had survived the fire, then maybe she really did have strange powers.

Katherine shrugged. "No one knows. She simply disappeared. She left behind a daughter, called Sara. Sara was brought up by the Silas Guppy of the time. He treated her as his own child and painted a picture of Rose for Sara to remember her mother by. When Sara grew up, she married and had a daughter, and passed on the painting to her."

"And she handed it on to *her* daughter, and so on, right down the years until *you* inherited it?" said Boz. "Amazing."

He and JJ stared into the painting, wondering what became of Reckless Rose herself. This was no ordinary picture. He had no doubt about that.

"My aunt is convinced that the picture is cursed," Katherine continued. "She thinks the curse has passed onto me because the picture is mine now. She believes that the curse is the revenge of the people of Dungeon Creek on the family of the woman who lured sailors to their doom . . . or so she says."

The room fell silent and Boz and JJ turned to stare into the fire. Watching the yellow and orange flames licking the small pile of logs, they thought back to the horrors of the days when people could be burned as witches and of the horrors of Rose's crimes.

Then Boz's thoughts returned to the painting with its strange Latin inscription. "Hang on," he gulped. "If the painting itself is cursed, and we now own it, that can only mean one thing. The curse has been passed on to us. *We're* cursed!"

The Stranger

"Nonsense!" said Mr. Barkis, his moonlit figure framed in the open doorway. "It's time that you went home Katherine. I'll drive you. Now, you two had better make yourself something to eat then go up to bed."

When Mr. Barkis got back from the house where Katherine lived with her Aunt Lilian, Boz and JJ were finishing their supper. "Don't start filling your heads with ideas about witches and curses," he said. "Katherine's aunt has a great deal to answer for. She thinks Katherine is in a wheelchair because of that stupid curse."

"That's ridiculous," said JJ in disbelief. "There are plenty of people in wheelchairs."

"You should see Katherine rowing a boat," said Boz. "She could beat me in a race anyday."

"Exactly," said Mr. Barkis. "Lilian Smallweed has some very outdated ideas. If I'd known this was the Reckless Rose picture, I'd have burned it the minute you brought it through that door . . ." His eyes lit up. "In fact, I think that's what I'll do right now."

Barkis snatched the oil painting and marched over to the fire. "No! Wait!" cried JJ. "Don't do that, Mr. Barkis. Surely it's for Katherine to decide what to do with the . . ."

But he was too late, or he would have been if something very strange hadn't happened. Before the painting reached the fireplace, a window crashed open and an incredible gust of wind blew into the room.

Papers were blown off a desk. A vase fell to the floor and shattered. And the flames of the fire were blown out in an instant.

The painting landed with a THUD in the harmless pile of ashes. JJ and Boz shuddered. For the first time since they'd arrived in Dungeon Creek, Mr. Barkis actually seemed slightly bothered. "Maybe it isn't right for me to destroy the painting," he mumbled. "Now, off to bed you two."

The next morning, Boz and JJ decided to return the painting to Katherine. Barkis told them the way to her house, and off they went. They took turns in carrying the painting because it had become strangely heavy.

As they were walking toward the village, a sleek black limousine pulled up alongside them. Even the windows were black, so they couldn't see inside. A very tall man stepped out of the car. He had strange eyes and a small pointed beard on the tip of his chin. His hair was silver. He reminded Boz of a goat.

The stranger blocked their path. He towered above them, staring over their heads into the distance. "You will give me the painting," he stated. His voice was strangely hypnotic. "NOW, " he added, as his eyes met theirs. They seemed to burn like red hot coals, and the boys began to feel scared.

Before Boz even had time to think, the man shot his arms out with lightning speed and snatched the painting from his grasp. He held their gaze for one moment longer, then leaped back into his car, barking an order to his driver. The limousine sped off at extremely high speed, leaving Boz and JJ trembling, with the stranger's gleeful laughter ringing in their ears.

A Confession and Confrontation

Not knowing what to do, JJ and Boz hurried to the house where Katherine lived with her Aunt Lilian. Once inside, they told Katherine and her aunt what had happened. Katherine was horrified by the description of the man.

"How terrible," she said. "He doesn't sound like anyone I know from around here – more like some spook in a horror movie."

"A stranger in Dungeon Creek," said Aunt Lilian mysteriously. "What would he be wanting with my Katherine's painting?"

"I thought you'd just be glad it's gone," said JJ. "After all, you did sell it to us to pass on the curse."

The woman blushed. "No, my dears. That's not quite right. I believe that the curse only falls on direct descendants of Reckless Rose. I thought that if I could sell it to someone outside the family who was willing to buy it, the curse would be broken. You haven't bought the curse, just a harmless old painting."

You boys have nothing to fear from the painting.

"What I want to know is how we can find the painting and get it back," said Boz . "Curse or no curse, Mrs. Smallweed, that is no ordinary painting. I'm sure . . . I'm sure that Reckless Rose is somehow trying to speak to me through it!" There was a stunned silence, only broken by a cry from JJ.

"Of course!" he cried. "It must have been goat-features who tried to steal the painting from the cottage the other night."

Lilian Smallweed's face turned an even deeper shade of red. "I have confession to make –" she began.

"It was you who broke into Mr. Barkis's cottage, wasn't it?" Katherine interrupted. "You were trying to steal the painting back. But why? I thought you'd be delighted to have it out of this house at last."

"I thought JJ and Boz were just passing through," she explained. "When I discovered that they were staying in Dungeon Creek, I realized that the painting would be too. I did it for *you*, Katherine."

Katherine spun her wheelchair around and headed down the hall for the front door. "You did it for me? You're crazy, Aunt Lilian. You're the one who believes in the curse, not me. Listen to yourself. You're not making any sense," she shouted. "One minute you say I'm 'saved' if the painting's sold. The next minute you say it has to leave the village! You don't know what to believe."

At that moment, without warning, the front door was thrown wide open.

Dazzling sunlight poured into the hallway. The brightness almost blinded them. Boz and JJ put their hands up to their faces to shield their eyes. "This is not what I want," said a familiar hypnotic voice. "You have tried to deceive me, children. What a very sad and foolish thing to do."

Something was thrown through the air and landed at Katherine's feet with a crash. It was the painting of Reckless Rose.

31

Unspoken Threats

As Boz and JJ's eyes became more used to the sunlight, they could make out the form of the frightening stranger. Though his voice was calm, his face was filled with rage. He didn't remind JJ of a goat anymore. He reminded him of a picture of a devil he'd seen somewhere. A picture that had given him terrifying nightmares.

"Oh, children," said the man. "Did you really think that you could trick me with this painting? In the original, the ship is much farther out to sea! This is a copy. A good copy, I'll grant you, but a fake."

I know who you are . . . I know you . .

Lilian Smallweed's jaw dropped wide open. She stared at the intruder but didn't do anything except mutter. She looked like an animal frozen with fear by the headlights of an oncoming car.

Katherine looked down at the painting. The man was right. The ship did look closer than before. "You can't fool me," she said. "You still have the original yourself. How dare you steal my painting then show up here with a fake. What's your game?" If she felt threatened by the man, it didn't show.

The stranger stormed over to the painting and snatched it up. "Don't lie to me, witch child. This is the picture the boys gave me. Look at the frame. Look at the back of the canvas," he snarled.

Is it the original?

The three children studied the picture. Everything about it was identical to the original, except that the ship was painted bigger so it looked nearer Reckless Rose and the shoreline.

Katherine glanced over to her aunt. Why wasn't she ordering this man out of their home? She simply sat there muttering: "You're Krowley. You're Doctor Krowley. I know your face . . . I know . . . "

JJ felt it was time to act. "If you don't leave right this second, I'll call the police. You're a thief and a bully," he said.

The stranger laughed his horrible laugh. "The police? Oh, foolish child. There are forces at work here that no police force in the world can stop! The old woman recognizes me, and speaks no words of disrespect. You should take a lesson from her. I shall be back, and I want the original painting. Clear?"

He didn't wait for an answer, but turned and walked out of the house, down the path and into his waiting black limousine.

"But this *is* the original painting," said Boz in amazement. He touched the figure of Reckless Rose. "I can sense it . . . I know it. Somehow, the ship really has moved. It looks bigger because it is getting closer to the rocks. In its own way, the picture is alive . . . " Behind him, Katherine's aunt let out a long and dreadful wail.

Back to the Lighthouse

They asked if anyone around the village had seen a goat-like stranger, or a black car, or knew anything about the name 'Doctor Krowley'. They drew a blank.

Ain't seen anyone like that 'round 'ere.

"He can't have vanished into thin air," said JJ.

"Why not?" said Boz glumly. "He looked a bit like a magician to me."

"He *is* very creepy," said his brother. "He wants the original painting and doesn't believe this is it. So what are we going to tell him when he comes back? He doesn't seem the type of man who would listen to reason."

"What worries me is that sooner or later, the man my aunt calls Krowley is going to discover his mistake. He'll realize that this *is* the original painting and that some strange force is making it change. Either way, we're in trouble," said Katherine, resting her chin in her hands.

They headed back to Mr. Barkis's cottage in silence for a while. Katherine had left Aunt Lilian tucked up in bed. The morning's events had seemed too much for her, but she'd refused any suggestions of calling a doctor.

"We're going to have to hide the painting," said JJ at last. "Somewhere that Krowley will never think of looking."

"I know the perfect place," said Katherine, her face breaking into a grin.

34

That night, Katherine rowed the two boys the short distance to the lighthouse. Boz and JJ jumped out of the boat and pulled it onto a smooth flat rock. They helped Katherine out of the boat to the front step of the lighthouse, where she sat down.

JJ went back to the boat and pulled out the painting, which Mr. Barkis had wrapped in an old blanket. Katherine's idea of bringing the painting here to hide it under cover of darkness seemed a good one.

Leaving Katherine to keep watch, Boz and JJ made their way up the stairs. They found the door to the circular room open. JJ leaned a chair against it to stop it blowing shut. "I wouldn't fancy having to swing through the downstairs window a second time," he said.

The sheets were still tied in position where they'd left them. They hauled them back in through the window. They didn't want anything odd catching Doctor Krowley's eye and attracting him to the lighthouse.

Before sliding it under the bed, they took one last look at the painting that was causing them so much trouble. The ship looked even bigger now. Yes, even closer to the treacherous rocks.

They hurried back down the stairs to Katherine, at least to where she should have been. She was nowhere in sight.

The boat was missing too. What was happening? Where had she gone, leaving them all alone?

"Where's Rose? Where's Rose?" screeched the myna bird, circling above them in the night sky.

Danger in the Dark

Boz shook his head in dismay. "It was a trick!" he moaned. "Katherine's left us stranded. I knew we should never have trusted her."

"Don't be so stupid," said JJ. "You're as bad as her aunt. What would be the point of leaving us here? When the tide goes out, we can walk back across the string of rocks."

"Then something must have happened to her," said Boz. They peered into the blackness of the night, following the sweeping beam of the lighthouse's huge lamp.

Less than a mile away, out to sea, Captain Weller of the cargo ship *Dickens* stepped into the wheelhouse of his ship and took over the helm. He turned the *Dickens* twenty degrees starboard. "We should be able to see the lighthouse soon," he said.

Meanwhile, Boz and JJ's hunt for Katherine was fruitless "I hope she's all right . . ." began JJ. At that moment there was a loud FIZZ and everything went pitch black. The huge revolving lamp at the top of the lighthouse had gone out.

"Great," sighed Boz. "That's all we need. That painting has even put a jinx on the lighthouse now."

Back on the *Dickens*, Captain Weller frowned. He was sure he had seen a flash of light, but now it was gone. It must have been lightning. He glanced down at his navigation chart. They would be reaching the dangerous coastline of Dungeon Creek soon. Thank heavens for the lighthouse to guide them.

At that same moment, on the rocks, JJ had a terrible thought. The lighthouse was there for a very special reason. It was there to warn ships away from the rocks. The danger was as great today as it had been in the time of the wreckers.

"Boz!" he cried, finding his brother's arm and grabbing it in the dark. "Can't you see what's happening? Reckless Rose is doing more than trying to speak to you through the painting. That witch is trying to reach out through the centuries to cause her first shipwreck in two hundred years! Maybe she's even using us to do it. We brought the painting here."

"But there aren't any ships around," began Boz. His words were drowned out by the deep and deafening sound of a ship's horn.

Unaware of the danger that lay ahead in the darkness, Captain Weller turned the helm of the *Dickens* and headed straight for the rocks of Dungeon Creek. The very rocks upon which Reckless Rose had stood two hundred years before.

MEUM TUM TIBI ADSTABO

Disaster on the Waves

Boz and JJ hurried up the winding dark staircase to the round room. Fumbling in the dark, they found the candles and matches that they remembered having seen in the trunk.

JJ tried striking several matches before one flared to life with a spluttering flame. The damp sea air hadn't helped, neither had his shaking hands.

They quickly lighted the candles, the faces of the many Silas Guppys stared from the wall, watching them in the eerie glow.

Now JJ and Boz had a far harder task. They had to try to get the huge light to work to warn the ship away from the rocks. Each holding a candle, they climbed the ladder to the lamp room.

In the middle of lamp room was what looked like an enormous electric globe, and a mechanism which was supposed to swivel around it to create the 'flashing' of the light. The mechanism was still, and the globe dead.

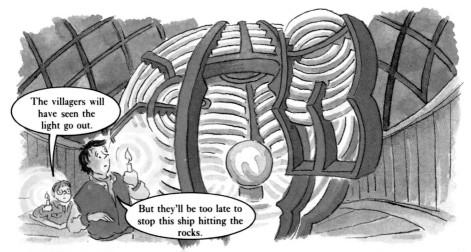

The villagers will have seen the light go out.

But they'll be too late to stop this ship hitting the rocks.

Around the outside of the room was a metal walkway, and huge glass windows overlooking both the land and sea.

JJ and Boz peered out into the night to see if they could spot the ship they'd heard. They dashed from one side to the other, straining their eyes in a frantic bid to find the vessel.

"There it is!" cried Boz, at last. He pointed to the *Dickens* moving toward them in the inky gloom. "Couldn't we light a fire in here to warn them?"

"By the time the flames are big enough for anyone to see, the ship will have been ripped to shreds on the rocks!" cried JJ. "And we brought the picture and its curse here. It's all our fault!"

In True Need

Boz and JJ hurried back down to the round room. "We only have one chance left," said Boz. "Our shouts will never be heard, and we can't get back to the village to get help. We'll have to try the painting."

"What? What do you mean?" asked JJ. "It's the painting that got us into this mess. Katherine's Aunt Lilian was right all along. It's cursed. It's evil."

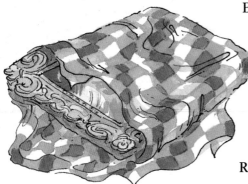

Boz pulled the painting out from its hiding place under the bed. It lay on the floor in front of them, still covered in a blanket. "Do you remember what the inscription said? *'If you truly need me, say my name and I shall be there to aid you.'* Don't you see, JJ? If we call out Reckless Rose's name, and really need her help, she will come to our aid. We can call her up. We can *summon* Reckless Rose to save the ship."

"Have you gone mad, Boz? It's a trick. It must be. Reckless Rose is probably causing all this trouble just so that you'll summon her up and let her loose on the world again," JJ argued. "If she can do all this when she's in a painting, think what she might be able to do if you call her up!"

"But she may have to do as we say if we summon her," said Boz. "Like a genie in a bottle . . . I don't know. We've got to try something, JJ."

Time was running out. The *Dickens* was drawing closer and closer to the rocks. Without the light of the Dungeon Creek lighthouse to guide it, Captain Weller and his crew had no idea that they were so far inland, so close to the jagged rocks, and so near disaster.

JJ pulled the blanket off the painting. In the strange glow of candlelight, the ship seemed enormous now, as though it was right by the rocks. Reckless Rose looked just the same as she always had . . . or was the expression on her face a little more triumphant?

"Right," said Boz, leaping to his feet. "I'm going to summon Rose now." As if on cue, the fog horn of the *Dickens* sounded once again – much louder and nearer this time. The brothers trembled, and the wind lashed against the tiny window, rattling it in its frame.

It's now or never.

Outside, the waves began to pound against the base of Dungeon Creek lighthouse, and seaspray battered against the glass of the lamp room. JJ was about to protest again, then caved in. "Maybe we can save that ship and its crew out there . . . or maybe all this is mumbo jumbo, so it won't make any difference anyway."

Just then, something caught JJ's eye. Something in the picture seemed to glint. He peered at it more closely. It was a row of tiny letters on the side of the ship. "Look. I've never seen these before!" he said.

"That's because the ship has never been close enough before. I told you that it was alive, didn't I?" cried Boz.

In amazement, the brothers read the name of the ship in the painting out loud. "The *Empress!*"

Moments later, there was a terrifying noise. It filled the air, and Dungeon Creek lighthouse shook to its very foundations.

41

From the Watery Grave

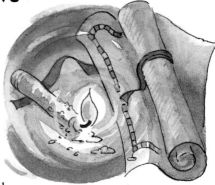

Boz and JJ rushed up to the lamp room. They wanted to see if the awful noise was the rocks ripping apart the hull of the cargo ship.

Below, a strange gust of wind blew a candle onto the floor. Its flame began to lick and burn the edge of an old navigation chart. Through the huge glass windows, they looked down at the scene out to sea. What they saw left them speechless.

The *Dickens* hadn't hit the rocks. It was still heading straight for them . . . What was making such an unnerving sound, filling the air around them? Between the ship and the rocks, there was a strange patch of water. . . glimmering . . . glowing. It was almost as if the moon itself was trapped beneath the waves, sending out its silvery light.

The shimmering water began to bubble like a witch's cauldron. Suddenly, an eerie ship with tattered sails broke through the surface of the waves with a resounding crash. Its ancient rigging creaked in the howling wind. Everywhere was bathed in a glowing silver light.

"'*If you truly need me, say my name and I shall be there to aid you*'," JJ yelled above the noise. "It wasn't Reckless Rose we could call out to for help. It was the ship in the painting. It was the *Empress*!"

On the bridge of the *Dickens*, the stunned captain couldn't believe his eyes. With a spin of the helm, he quickly changed course to avoid the eerie sight, and steered his rusting vessel away from the danger of the hidden rocks of Dungeon Creek.

Scuppered Plans

From their vantage point up in the lamp room, Boz and JJ stood, open mouthed, watching the miraculous events unfold below them. The night sky was illuminated by the silvery glow of the *Empress*. Then, and only then, did they spot something else. A small speedboat, bobbing anchored in the water. Someone else had witnessed these extraordinary events.

Katherine's tiny boat was attached to the speedboat by a rope. In the front of the speedboat stood Dr. Krowley. He was staring at the shimmering *Empress*, a mad glint in his eyes.

"He must have followed us here and kidnapped Katherine when we went upstairs," groaned Boz. "He'll probably keep her prisoner until we give him the painting. He certainly knows something about its power . . . and will obviously stop at nothing until he gets it. That man is pure evil."

Dr. Krowley turned his head and stared straight up at the top of the lighthouse where the brothers were still standing. Although they couldn't even see his eyes from that distance, they somehow felt his penetrating gaze. He threw his head back like a wolf howling at the moon and began to shout into the night.

JJ and Boz hurried onto a small balcony which ran around the outside of the lamp room, and caught Krowley's words in the wind. "I have the witch child, now I must have the power of the painting!" he wailed.

Some of Krowley's words were drowned out by the crashing waves, or were lost when the wind changed direction. In these moments, he seemed even more enraged, like some villain in a silent film with a fist raised in anger.

The words that came through loud and clear made Boz and JJ shudder. "I know that you are up there boys. Distance and darkness do not hinder my sight. You have something I want or who knows what might happen to your poor little friend here?"

JJ and Boz knew that they would have to let him have the painting. All that mattered was that Katherine should be released unharmed.

What Krowley didn't notice was that his prisoner, Katherine, was pulling herself forward. JJ and Boz watched as she lifted up one of the oars from her boat and swung it straight at him.

The edge of the oar hit the back of Krowley's knees. With the roar of an injured animal, he toppled headfirst into the silver sea. At that precise moment, there was a deafening BOOM, followed by a splintering of glass. Sparks began to fly around the lamp room.

A Few Days Later

"It's funny how newspapers always come up with such ordinary explanations for such extraordinary events," said JJ looking at the clippings Katherine was sticking in a scrapbook.

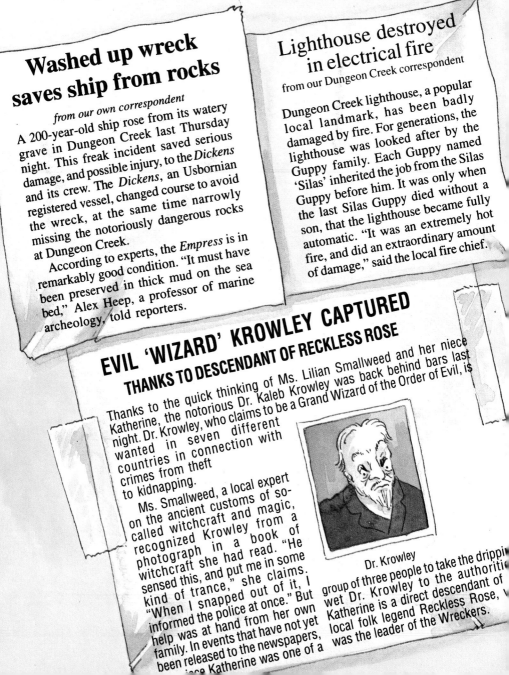

Washed up wreck saves ship from rocks

from our own correspondent

A 200-year-old ship rose from its watery grave in Dungeon Creek last Thursday night. This freak incident saved serious damage, and possible injury, to the *Dickens* and its crew. The *Dickens*, an Usbornian registered vessel, changed course to avoid the wreck, at the same time narrowly missing the notoriously dangerous rocks at Dungeon Creek.

According to experts, the *Empress* is in remarkably good condition. "It must have been preserved in thick mud on the sea bed," Alex Heep, a professor of marine archeology, told reporters.

Lighthouse destroyed in electrical fire

from our Dungeon Creek correspondent

Dungeon Creek lighthouse, a popular local landmark, has been badly damaged by fire. For generations, the lighthouse was looked after by the Guppy family. Each Guppy named 'Silas' inherited the job from the Silas Guppy before him. It was only when the last Silas Guppy died without a son, that the lighthouse became fully automatic. "It was an extremely hot fire, and did an extraordinary amount of damage," said the local fire chief.

EVIL 'WIZARD' KROWLEY CAPTURED
THANKS TO DESCENDANT OF RECKLESS ROSE

Thanks to the quick thinking of Ms. Lilian Smallweed and her niece Katherine, the notorious Dr. Kaleb Krowley was back behind bars last night. Dr. Krowley, who claims to be a Grand Wizard of the Order of Evil, is wanted in seven different countries in connection with crimes from theft to kidnapping.

Ms. Smallweed, a local expert on the ancient customs of so-called witchcraft and magic, recognized Krowley from a photograph in a book of witchcraft she had read. "He sensed this, and put me in some kind of trance," she claims. "When I snapped out of it, I informed the police at once." But help was at hand from her own family. In events that have not yet been released to the newspapers, [...]ce Katherine was one of a

Dr. Krowley

group of three people to take the dripp[...] wet Dr. Krowley to the authoriti[...] Katherine is a direct descendant of local folk legend Reckless Rose, [...] was the leader of the Wreckers.

"And there's no mention of our brave efforts to warn that ship, or Katherine bringing the boat alongside the lighthouse when the fire broke out," said Boz. "But they've made your aunt out to be some kind of a hero." He laughed.

"I'm just happy it all ended well," said Katherine. "The painting wasn't a force for evil, but a force for good. Aunt Lilian was quite wrong."

The other two nodded. "The Silas Guppy who painted the picture and gave it to Rose's daughter was somehow trying to bring *good* luck to your family," said Boz. "Perhaps to give them a chance to do something right after all of Reckless Rose's wrong-doings."

"Warning the *Dickens* and clobbering Krowley was certainly the right thing to do," added JJ.

"I may be in a wheelchair, but I'm no pushover," said Katherine. "He's the one who was pushed over . . . over*board*." They all laughed. She closed the scrapbook.

"It's a shame that the painting was destroyed in the fire," said Boz. "I suppose once it had served its purpose . . ." He shrugged.

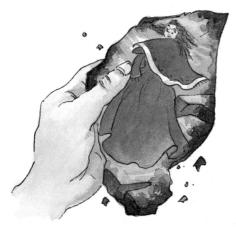

"The painting wasn't entirely destroyed," said Katherine. From under the scrapbook she produced the only remaining piece of the painting and passed it to Boz and JJ.

It was just a small piece of the canvas, with charred edges. On it was Reckless Rose. There wasn't so much as a speck of soot on her. She was entirely undamaged. Once again, the so-called witch of Dungeon Creek had escaped the flames.

Did You Spot?

You can use this page to help spot things that could be useful in solving the mystery. First, there are hints and clues you can read as you go along. They will give you some idea of what to look out for. Then there are extra notes to read which tell you more about what happened afterwards.

Hints and Clues

3   Look at the items on the stall carefully. You may come across some similar objects later on.

4-5   Try to familiarize yourself with the painting.

6-7   Remember what the intruder is wearing, and keep your eyes peeled.

8-9   Shadows can reveal a great deal about a person.

10-11   Familiar names and familiar figures.

12-13   Something in the grass might raise its ugly head in the not too distant future.

14-15   Think about Silas Guppy. There must be a simple solution.

16-17   It's worth remembering the things in the old chest. Something could come in handy later on.

18-19   Are there any familiar faces in this tale?

20-21   Look closely. Is help at hand?

22-23   Katherine probably knows more than she is prepared to say at present.

24-25   Mr. Barkis has a few familiar objects in his workshop. Look closely.

26-27   Wreckers and witches? This must be of some importance.

28-29   The stick that the goat-like stranger is carrying has appeared somewhere before.

34-35   The myna bird has something strange to say.

36-37   If Katherine hasn't gone off on her own, who might have taken her? And why?

40-41   Boz and JJ have said the name of the ship in the painting. That must be important.

42-43   Everything should be falling into place by now.

In the End

There was a reward for the capture of Dr. Krowley. Katherine spent some of the money buying a better wheelchair, designed for getting about faster.

The only remaining piece of the painting is now in a glass case in Dungeon Creek Museum.

Mr. Barkis was interviewed by local police about his fake antiques being sold as the real thing. It turned out that he knew nothing about it. He had sold them as copies to a man from the city.

When foundations were laid to build the new lighthouse, the builders found an old skeleton. Katherine thinks that they are the bones of Reckless Rose, found at last after two hundred years.

The myna bird, that JJ has now named 'Beakie', is a direct descendant of the myna bird owned by the Silas Guppy who painted Reckless Rose.

By the Way ...

Did you spot:

It was Aunt Lilian casting the shadow on page 9.

Krowley dropped his stick outside the lighthouse before Boz and JJ visited it for the first time.

The jail Reckless Rose was held in was an old cave with bars set into the rock. This was the old dungeon which Dungeon Creek was named after.

STAGE FRIGHT

Paul Stewart

Illustrated by Alan Marks

Designed by Lucy Smith

Edited by Phil Roxbee Cox

Contents

A Strange Encounter

Thunder rumbled ominously as Dom approached the impressive wrought-iron gates that barred the way to Mask Manor. He peered through the railings. In the failing light, he could just make out the house where he was to spend the next two weeks. He shuddered.

Without warning, feathers brushed against his face . . . but Dom could see nothing. What was happening? The sound of flapping wings filled the air all around him. He screamed, then screamed again. What felt like vicious claws and beaks were scraping at his skin.

Desperately raising his arms for protection, Dom stumbled. He fell against the gates, which creaked open behind him. As he tumbled inside, the attack came to an abrupt halt. "H-Help me," he cried.

Welcome to Mask Manor

Seconds later, a man appeared by the roadside, as if from nowhere. "The village is that way," he said to Dom, and pointed with a bony finger.

"But I'm staying here at the manor," Dom explained, brushing gravel from his jeans. The stranger's expression changed and Dom's stomach churned with foreboding. "My aunt invited me . . ." he began.

"Oh, so you're *related* to them, are you?" the man interrupted, spitting out the word. And with that, he was gone.

Dom stared into the darkness after him. He touched his stinging cheek. There was blood on his fingers. As the huge gates swung shut behind him, Dom realized that he was trembling. What had his parents let him in for, he wondered, as he crunched his way up the drive.

He arrived at the huge front door of Mask Manor and pressed an ancient bell. Instantly, the door was flung wide open, and a stern-faced woman glared out at him. "Who are you?" she demanded. "What do you want?" It was getting even darker now and rain had begun to fall. A distant bell rang out.

"Hello," said Dom as cheerfully as he could. "Aunt Eloise? I'm Dom – " Seeing the look of surprise on the woman's face, he broke off. "You *are* Mrs. Eloise Bound, aren't you?"

"Indeed I am," she said. "But what makes you think I'm your aunt?"

Dom was confused. What had his mother told him? Eloise Bound was married to one of Dad's second cousins once removed. Or was it one of his first cousins twice removed? He frantically tried to remember. "Er, you called yourself aunt in your letter, so I thought – "

"What letter?" the woman interrupted with annoyance. "I never wrote to anyone." Dom pulled a crumpled piece of paper from his pocket. The woman snatched it from him. Reading it quickly, her eyes widened. "This looks like my typing all right . . . and it's certainly my signature . . . but I never wrote this. At least . . . well, such odd things have been happening lately . . ."

Dom sighed. He had been excited when his aunt's letter had arrived. It had suggested two weeks at Mask Manor, with tennis courts, a swimming pool and stables – not that he was interested in the "darling little ponies" that were mentioned. The letter had made the place sound warm and inviting. Dom now strongly suspected otherwise.

"Dom?" The woman frowned, then her expression changed. "Dom!" she cried. "Yes, *of course*, I'm your Aunt Eloise. Welcome to Mask Manor . . ." She showed him in. "What have you done to your face?" she added.

Dom didn't feel able to share the attack at the gates with this peculiar aunt who couldn't even remember having invited him. "I tripped," he lied. He found himself standing in a huge, gloomy hallway.

"Then be more careful," she said, tugging a dusty bell-pull. Dom could make out a muffled clanging in some far off corner of the house. "Now listen. I must go upstairs. When Mildred appears, get her to take you up to the Blue Room," Aunt Eloise instructed. Then her voice went oddly dreamy. "I mean the Paisley Room," she said. "Get her to make you up a bed in the Paisley Room."

Meet the Family

Dom left his suitcase in the Paisley Room with its nightmare wallpaper of swirling patterns. Supper, he'd been told, was in ten minutes. Making his way down the corridor, Dom heard raised voices.

As he passed a door, he clearly heard his name mentioned. The door was ajar and Dom couldn't help but overhear what was being said. There were two voices – Aunt Eloise's and a man's. They both sounded angry.

"Something evil is afoot," Aunt Eloise was saying. "I can *feel* it. First my painting, now the letter and this child," she cried. "Nothing must get in the way of our plan. *Nothing*."

"Be patient!" snapped the man. "We mustn't drop our guard now, with only three more days to go."

Three more days? Three more days until what, Dom wondered. He saw his aunt heading for the door, so hurried back down the corridor to his room.

A few minutes later, Dom crossed a gallery overlooking a dreary dining room. Beneath a dusty chandelier, sat the inhabitants of Mask Manor. Dom took one look at them and shuddered. He didn't want to sit with them, but where else could he go? He hurried downstairs and sat at the only empty place at the table.

Begrudgingly, Aunt Eloise introduced him to the assembled company. "The bald man is my loving husband, your Uncle Giles. The other man is his brother, your Uncle Charles." She nodded in the direction of a man staring ahead of him, as if in a trance. He was being spoon-fed by a woman. "And this is your Uncle Charles's nurse, Isobel Beauchamp. She only eats with us because someone has to feed him. "

"My brother Charles has been in this sad and sorry state for over a year," Dom's Uncle Giles explained. "It happened at a variety show. He went on stage to help a h– "

"To help in a magic trick," Eloise butted in. "It was a tragedy. A rope snapped, a sandbag fell from the ceiling . . . and since then your Uncle Charles has been as you see him now," she said. "Worthless. A waste of space."

Deaf to their conversation, Charles continued to chew what Isobel was feeding him. It appeared to be a slimy mixture of raw meat and egg. Dom felt physically sick.

"It's odd," Aunt Eloise mused. "Once Charles was considered to be the lucky brother. He had it all. Charm, looks, hair . . ." She sneered at Giles.

"I was born hairless," Giles interrupted. "Apart from eyebrows, of course." It was *his* voice Dom had heard upstairs with Aunt Eloise.

". . . and business sense," Eloise went on. "But business hasn't been so good for Charles's company since this latest accident. Of course, we've tried everything in our power to get him well again, but . . ." she broke off and shuddered.

Dom felt an icy wind. He had the horrible feeling that someone was watching him. The sound of breaking glass suddenly shattered the silence. Eloise had knocked over her wine. The red liquid spread out over the table cloth like blood.

A Message from Beyond

After supper, Dom went straight up to his room but he couldn't sleep. Outside, a storm raged and a branch scraped at the window like someone trying to get in. It was no comfort knowing that the Bounds were sitting below. He was so alone, yet still felt as though he was being watched. It was eerie.

Suddenly, a desolate howl echoed around the manor. Dom sat bolt upright. What was that? He trembled. It sounded just like he imagined a hungry wolf would sound. More than a little nervous, Dom switched on the light. He regretted it at once. Looking at the swirly wallpaper made him dizzy.

"Two weeks in this terrible place," Dom groaned. He reached for his clock and pressed the switch that made it work as a calculator. He began tapping the keys. "Two weeks is 14 days which is 336 hours, which is . . . 1,209,600 seconds. Now, minus the time I've been here . . . Hold on!" Dom stared at the calculator which was beginning to take on a life of its own. As he stared, a sequence of numbers flashed on the display, over and over again:

"Can't anything be normal in this place?" he muttered, trying to switch the gadget back to being a clock. The sequence of numbers continued. Dom switched it off. The numbers kept flashing. He tossed it onto the bed, where it lay peep-peeping insistently. And still the numbers flashed. Unable to tear his eyes away, Dom stared with motionless horror. Without even knowing why, he reached forward and picked up the gadget. Then, as if in slow motion, he turned it around in his hand.

Realization dawned. Upside down, the numbers formed letters! Snatching a pen and paper from his bedside table, he carefully wrote down each word in the order they kept on appearing.

He frowned. What did they all mean? Lies . . . Lies . . . Mask Manor was certainly a house of lies, what with Aunt Eloise claiming she hadn't even sent him the letter inviting him there.

ELOISE
LIES
GILES
LIES
SEE
ISOBEL.

Suddenly, Dom felt sure that he knew the calculator's meaning. It was some kind of message. No. It was more than that. It was some kind of *warning*. But who from?

The words began swimming around inside his head . . . His eyelids became heavy . . . he drifted into a deep, deep sleep. Dom began to dream . . . A little girl stood before him and began to change shape. Her eyes slid around to the side of her head, and her nose grew hard and pointed. The girl lifted her arms as they sprouted feathers and twisted back to form wings . . . Unable to scream or turn away, Dom was being forced to watch the girl turn into a bird.

The Playhouse Beckons

The next morning, by the light of day, things didn't seem quite so bad. Dom decided to explore the grounds. He was eager to take his mind off the events of the night before.

It was soon clear that the gardens had been neglected. Everything needed weeding, pruning or mowing. As for the swimming pool, it was choked with duckweed. Dom decided to explore the nearby village instead.

Although pretty, the village seemed to be a sleepy place. It was dominated by a large, ugly red brick building with boarded-up windows.

THE MASK PLAYHOUSE

MESMO THE MAGNIFICENT

A torn poster advertised what must have been one of the Playhouse's last performances, a 'variety show'. Two enormous eyes stared out. As Dom passed, their intense gaze seemed to follow him. Dom stared back, and his head began to reel. Suddenly, he felt that he must go inside the building . . . He just had to . . .

Dom walked down the side of the Mask Playhouse to a door that he somehow *knew* would be there, and would be unlocked. It was a fire exit, so there was no handle on the outside. He levered it open with his fingertips and stepped inside. He pushed open a door at the end of a passage, and found himself in a dusty, yet magnificent, auditorium. "This must be where my Uncle Charles had his accident up on stage," he said, surprising himself by speaking out loud.

"You're quite right, of course," said a voice. Dom spun around. It was Isobel Beauchamp, his Uncle Charles's nurse. "What brings you to the Mask Playhouse?" she asked quietly. "Have you been drawn to it?"

"I – I don't know," Dom confessed. "It looked interesting and here I am."

"Then perhaps I didn't need to tempt you with the darling little ponies," said Isobel softly.

Darling little ponies? Where had Dom come across those very words before? Of course, in the letter. "You sent me that letter and signed it in my aunt's name, didn't you?" he exclaimed. "You invited me to this awful place. No wonder Aunt Eloise couldn't remember writing it!" Isobel Beauchamp nodded. "But why?" Dom demanded. "Why all of these lies?"

"I need help," said Isobel. "Not just for me but . . . " she paused, ". . . for the others. Please meet me at the summerhouse at two o'clock. I'll explain everything then." With that, she turned and hurried out of sight.

Dom was about to call out to her when something caught his eye. A fluttering of wings? No. A yellowing piece of paper, floating lazily from the rafters. He put out his hand and it landed directly in his palm. It was a newspaper clipping, almost ten years old.

CLOSE SHAVE FOR BUDDING ACTOR

Rising star, Simon Steele, was 'seriously wounded' following an accident on stage during a 'one night only' performance of *Hamlet,* according to eye-witness Larry 'the lamp' Watkins. It happened at the reopened Mask Playhouse.

Steele (25) was to have played the leading role of Hamlet himself but, following a minor throat infection, agreed to switch to the less important role of Polonius at the last minute.

It was as Polonius that Simon Steele was stabbed and injured. Mr. Watkins, the

Larry Watkins

Playhouse's lighting electrician, told reporters: 'The trick sword must have jammed. It was an accident I suppose, but my heart goes out to Simon Steele. He's lucky to be alive. This was a terrible thing to happen.' The Mask Playhouse was recently restored thanks to the money and effort of local businessman, Mr. Charles Bound of Mask Manor.

The Story Unfolds

Newspaper clipping in hand, Dom left the Mask Playhouse and was heading back along the alley when he walked slam-bang into someone coming the other way. It was the stranger he had met in front of the gates of Mask Manor the night before.

The man looked at Dom in surprise, then strode off. There was something about his face which puzzled Dom. He glanced back down at the newspaper story. That was it! The beard was gone, but there was no doubt. The man in the photograph was the man in front of him now. He was none other than Larry 'the lamp' Watkins, who had been the Playhouse's lighting electrician.

Without pausing to think, Dom called out after him. "Mr. Watkins? Please wait. Can I talk to you?"

The man turned. "How do you know my name?" he asked. "What have they been saying about me up at the Manor?"

"Nothing, Mr. Watkins," said Dom, catching up with him. He handed the old man the newspaper story. "I wanted to ask you about this."

Larry Watkins glanced down at the clipping. "Oh, the accident with the sword in *Hamlet*. What about it?" he asked. "I thought you were going to ask me about the other accident."

"Uncle Charles's accident?" Dom asked. "Please Mr. Watkins, I need to talk to *someone* about what's been going on around here. I'm so confused."

"Mask Manor is a bad place," sighed Mr. Watkins. "And the Mask Playhouse has brought nothing but trouble." He began walking on, and Dom kept up beside him. "I should have warned you," he said. They reached a small cottage where a pink-cheeked woman was in the garden, busy picking roses. "Mavis," he said. "This is the boy I told you about. I bumped into him again. This time at the Playhouse."

"The Playhouse?" said Mavis, leading them into a room packed with theatrical props. "My Larry has an incredible collection of things from there. Have a look while we make some tea." The old pair shuffled out of the room.

Dom flicked through a pile of leaflets. Quite by chance – or so it seemed at the time – he found a cast list for the 'one night only' performance of *Hamlet*. A typewritten note had been clipped to it. Dom's eyes widened. "According to this, my Uncle Charles played Hamlet on the night that Simon Steele was stabbed!" said Dom, when Mr. and Mrs. Watkins had returned with the tea.

Larry Watkins nodded. "Yes. Charles Bound is – was – remarkable," he said. "He was always such an amazingly hard worker. No one was surprised when his business was such a success. He deserved it." The old man sipped his tea. "He did so much for the village too."

"Unlike his brother Giles, who was always off on his crazy expeditions," added Mrs. Watkins. "Until he married Eloise and settled down back at the manor a few months ago."

"It was Charles who restored the Mask Playhouse to its former glory," Mr. Watkins continued. "He not only saved the building, he saved the show, too – more than once. He was trying to save it by playing Hamlet that night. Simon Steele wasn't well enough to take the lead role, so Charles stepped in at the last minute and took his place . . . "

"And ended up stabbing poor Steele," said Mrs. Watkins. "Jinxed. The place is jinxed. Now, it's time you were on your way, Dom," she added rather abruptly. Dom thanked them both and left.

61

Birds at the Window

Although Dom took a shortcut through the woods, it was a little after two o'clock when he emerged in the grounds of Mask Manor. He was late for his appointment with Isobel Beauchamp.

Dom saw at once that their agreed meeting place, the octagonal summerhouse, was empty.

Dom hoped that he hadn't missed her. He decided to wait. Around the walls of the summerhouse was a bench with built-in cupboards underneath. Dom passed the time by exploring them. Behind each door he found souvenirs of happier times at Mask Manor – an old sunhat, empty lemonade bottles, croquet mallets . . .

Suddenly, a loud 'CRASH' made Dom jump up in surprise. He spun around and saw at once what had made the noise. A magpie had flown against a window with such force that it had cracked the glass.

"Poor thing," he said and rushed over to the door to see if the creature was all right. Before his hand had even reached the handle, he stopped dead in his tracks. His heart began to pound furiously. The bird was not alone. In all, there were eight of them. Eight birds. Instinctively, Dom touched his cheek where he had been scratched by invisible beaks and claws the day before.

As if frozen to the spot, Dom stared in horror as the birds began tap-tap-tapping on the glass with their beaks. As one, they beat out a curious rhythm. On and on it went . . . again and again. Each sharp tap on the glass seemed to penetrate deep into Dom's brain.

"Stop it! Stop!" he screamed. "Why are you doing this to me? Why?"

Into the Void

As Dom stood mesmerized by the birds' insistent tapping, the summerhouse began to revolve. It turned slowly at first, then accelerated until the lawn, the trees and Mask Manor itself were like a smudge of paint smeared across the windows.

It was like the most terrifying fairground ride gone terribly wrong. The summerhouse was spinning, faster and faster and faster, twirling and swirling . . . spinning . . . spinning . . . Dom found himself pulled off his feet and flung against a window. Pinned there, unable to move, he prayed that the glass wouldn't break.

Still the tapping went on. The same pattern, over and over. And, as it repeated, Dom heard the faint sound of children's voices, chanting in time with the beat:

"Ring around the roses,
A pocket full
of posies.
Ashes! Ashes!
We all fall down!"

"Ring-a-ring-a-roses
A pocket full of posies.
A-tishoo! A-tishoo!
We all fall . . . DOWN!"

As the final word rang out, the summerhouse seemed to explode in a shower of glass. Dom found himself hurtling down into a dark tunnel, studded with stars and filled with the sound of giggling children.

Lightning cracked all around him and, for a split second, Dom saw what the 'stars' really were. Try as he might, he was unable to stop himself crying out in sheer terror. They were the glinting beaks and gleaming claws of cold-eyed birds. "NO!" he screamed.

64

As another sheet of lightning lit up his surroundings, Dom now saw fingers at the birds' wing tips, beckoning . . . beckoning . . . A wren appeared. It seemed to be clutching a pulsating disk in its tiny claws.

"Seek the talisman," whispered a voice deep inside Dom. He reached out to grab the disk but his hand passed straight through it and his outstretched fingers closed around nothing but thin air. He tumbled away into the darkness.

Cries of despair filled the void and faded away, until all Dom could hear was one plaintive voice whispering to him from the darkness. "I want to come home," it pleaded. "Please help me. Please help me to come home!"

Weird Works of Art

Dom opened his eyes and looked blearily around the summerhouse. It was still in one piece. What was happening? With a sudden shock, he saw that he wasn't alone. A girl was kneeling next to him. "Who are you?" he exclaimed.

"Abi," said the girl. "Abi Watkins. I live with my granny and grandpa. I was told to stay upstairs when you came because Grandpa doesn't like me meeting anyone from the manor," she explained. "But I'd seen you snooping around the Playhouse and wondered what you were up to."

Dom sighed. He was relieved to meet someone around his own age, and with a friendly face, too. "Something very weird is going on around here, Abi," he said. "I was supposed to be meeting someone who might be able to explain part of it, but she hasn't shown up." Then – without really knowing why – he told Abi everything that had happened since his arrival at Mask Manor, from the odd letter of invitation, to what had just happened in the summerhouse.

To his surprise, Abi didn't scoff. "So much has changed since Grandpa used to bring me up here to the manor," she said. "I used to play here with a girl called Jenny Beauchamp . . ."

"Beauchamp?" Dom interrupted. "That's Isobel's name. Who's Jenny? Her daughter? There are no children staying at the manor, apart from me."

"Jenny's not here any more . . . Nobody knows where she is and Grandpa says that the police have given up looking. She disappeared on the day of that awful variety show . . . The day my grandpa was arrested and the Playhouse closed down again." Abi looked away. "I must go," she said wiping her eyes. "Granny and Grandpa worry about me. I'll see you soon."

That evening, Dom found himself eating alone but not in silence. Mildred, the maid who had shown him to his room the night before, now appeared with a plate of cold meat. She seemed to want to talk *at* him all the time. "On your own tonight, Dominic," she cackled, plonking the plate in front of him. "Your Uncle Charles is in bed, Mrs. Beauchamp is in the village and them other two are at the casino. It's incredible the amount of time they spend gambling."

"Really?" said Dom, thoughtfully studying the meat. He was starving. In all the excitement and confusion, he'd missed lunch.

"Mind you," Mildred went on. "Things were a mess when I was taken on ten years ago. Flora, the housekeeper, had been fired for some wrong doing. It was just me and your Uncle Charles here then. He lived on his own after he stabbed that actor at his precious Playhouse. Poor man. Look at him now." She bustled out and didn't return.

With everyone now out of the way, Dom decided to explore the house. He found himself making his way up a flight of stairs and into a large, airy studio. It was as if his feet had simply led him there. The initials on some of the pictures suggested that they'd been painted by Aunt Eloise. Looking around at these childish works, Dom decided that he could paint better than that when he was *three*.

Something drew Dom's eyes to a painting on an easel. He shuddered as he recognized the familiar patterned circle. It was the same as the disk the wren had been holding out to him.

As he stood there, the painted circle began spinning around . . . around . . . around . . . Try as he might, he could not look away. A voice inside his head was instructing him to stare deep into the circle. Dom had no choice but to obey.

67

The Fateful Performance

In a state somewhere between wakefulness and sleep, Dom began walking. It was dark, but his feet never once stumbled. Automatically, they turned this way and that. Now left. Now right. Taking him back to the Mask Playhouse!

Stepping inside was like stepping into the heart of an old black and white movie, without actually being a part of the action. The Playhouse was packed with people. Up on the stage, a magician was holding the audience with his dark eyes – eyes which Dom recognized from the poster. What was his name? Mesmo. Of course, that was it – Mesmo the Magnificent.

A man and girl were making their way up from the front row to the stage. There was no mistaking that it was Uncle Charles. But not the Uncle Charles that Dom had met. He was laughing and joking. This was Charles *before* his accident. In the front row, next to two empty seats, sat Isobel. She too looked different. Happier. Was the little girl on stage her daughter, Jenny?

As if grasped by invisible hands, Dom's head was twisted upward. He found himself staring up at Abi's grandpa, Larry Watkins, adjusting a spotlight up on the catwalk. But this was not all Dom was meant to see. His gaze was drawn into the dark shadows. Someone else was up there, too!

Back on stage, Mesmo was flashing a light into Uncle Charles's eyes. He spoke but, to Dom, the words kept fading in and out. He couldn't make head nor tail of what was being said. With a sickening jolt, Dom realized that the little girl, Jenny, was nowhere to be seen. Where could she have gone?

Mesmo clicked his fingers. Charles dropped onto all fours in a trance and prowled around the stage like an animal. Then, without warning, a sandbag struck Mesmo on the side of his head. The entire audience jumped up in horror. Then the lights went out. The performance had come to an abrupt end.

When the lights came on again, Dom found himself back in Aunt Eloise's studio. He blinked. His head was spinning. He'd just been through a playback of the past and – if what he'd seen was the truth – he'd had things confused. He'd assumed that his Uncle Charles was the one who had been hit by a sandbag. But it had been Mesmo. So what had happened to his uncle? Dom frowned. That was it! *Uncle Charles must still be stuck in the trance.*

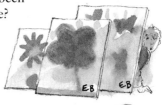

Dom was interrupted by voices coming up the stairs. Without a second thought, he hid behind some paintings leaning up against a wall.

69

Invisible Attack!

Uncle Giles burst into the studio and threw his coat onto the back of a chair. "Ten thousand. You lost ten thousand, all on the last spin of the wheel!" he exclaimed. "It makes me want to scream."

"I can do without your childish tantrums, thank you," snapped Eloise. "I thought you said that you weren't in this for the money but for the revenge. The money is a bonus." She rummaged in her handbag and produced a large key. "Anyway, there's plenty more where that came from, thanks to your dear *brother*," she said, and laughed.

Giles stared sulkily at the picture that had had such a hypnotic effect on Dom. "Perhaps you should spend some of our ill-gotten gains on painting lessons," he scoffed. "What is *that* supposed to be?"

Eloise shrugged. "I don't even remember painting it," she confessed, unlocking a safe in the wall. Dom could see neat bundles of money stacked inside. His aunt grinned and patted the largest bundle. This was the first time Dom had seen her looking happy.

"It sort of happened when I was painting yesterday afternoon."

"That must be why it looks better than your usual floral efforts," Giles laughed. The sound died in his throat. "Aaargh!" he cried.

Giles's face was fixed with an expression of sheer terror. He threw his arms up as if to protect himself from the painting on the easel . . . or from some invisible beast leaping from the picture.

"Keep that dog away from me!" he screamed. "Get it away! You know how I hate dogs!"

Giles was shaking with fear. Whatever he could see, or thought he could see, was driving him out of his mind.

70

Dom couldn't see a dog from his hiding place, and it was obvious Aunt Eloise saw nothing either. "I could do without one of your over-theatrical performances at the moment," she snapped. "Save your energy for your role in the grand finale in the library."

But Giles was deaf to her insults. His eyes bulged and his teeth chattered as he staggered from the invisible terror. "No . . ." he whimpered. "NO!"

Suddenly there was a loud 'CRASH' as he stumbled against the easel. The picture clattered to the floor, with Giles not far behind.

Giles and the easel lay in an unceremonious heap. "Where's it gone?" he moaned, sitting up and looking around the studio with a puzzled frown. Eloise strode over to him and stood there, hands on hips.

"Where's *what* gone? Your mind?" she demanded. "Now get up. There are only two more days to go and I'm not about to let you ruin everything by falling apart on me now!"

"Sorry," said Giles, getting to his feet. "It was so real. I – I don't know what to think. But don't worry. I won't let you down. I've waited so long for this, and revenge such as this is well worth waiting for!"

Isobel's Secret

Back in his room at last, Dom lay awake in bed. It was clear that Uncle Giles and Aunt Eloise were up to something, but how was it connected to the birds, or the accidents at the Playhouse? His mind kept on coming back to a jammed theatrical sword and a falling sandbag.

A thought suddenly struck Dom. He sat bolt upright. When he had experienced the strange playback of events at the Mask Playhouse, *Isobel Beauchamp had been in the audience.* And what had Abi Watkins, the girl at the summerhouse, said? That she used to play with Jenny Beauchamp at the manor . . . but Isobel had been introduced as Uncle Charles's nurse. So why would he need a nurse *before* the accident that left him in a trance?

When Dom finally tracked down Isobel the next morning, she had a strange story to tell. As she spoke, he pictured the events clearly in his mind . . .

1. After the accident with the sword in *Hamlet*, your Uncle Charles hid himself away. For nine years he lived like a recluse.
   "I could have killed Simon!"

2. Fate was to change all that. Jenny and I were taking a break. The first since Jenny's father died.
   "I'm afraid we're lost, Jenny."

3. Jenny spotted Mask Manor and I decided to ask for help.
   "Can you help us, please?"
   "What do you want from me?"

4. Charles let us in, reluctantly. He let us spend the night in the guest wing . . . then the next night . . .
   "I never want to leave here. I like Charles."

5. To cut a long story short, your uncle and I decided to marry . . .
   "I'm so happy."
   "Me too!"

6. . . . and to celebrate by reopening the Playhouse and putting on a variety show.
   "For a finale, we'll get up on stage and reveal to the whole world that we're getting married!"

Isobel was fighting back the tears when she had finished her tale. "There's something you must promise me, Dom," she said. "Your Uncle Giles and Aunt Eloise don't know about Charles and me. When Giles returned – after years away – with his new wife, Eloise, it was easier to say that I was Charles's nurse. You must promise not to tell them."

"I promise," said Dom solemnly. "But why did you lie, Mrs. Beauchamp?"

"Simple," said Isobel. "Charles and I kept our engagement a secret. No one knew about it but us. With Charles the way he is now, it would be my word against anyone else's. More than anything, I want to be with him. I want to help him. But your aunt and uncle might think that I'm some money-grabber trying to lay claim to your Uncle Charles's money . . . "

Mysterious Consequences

Dom and Isobel were conducting their secret conversation in the stables. Suddenly, Aunt Eloise's face appeared at the stable door. Dom's heart skipped a beat. How long had she been outside? Had she been eavesdropping? "Oh there you are, *dear*," she said with a forced jolliness in her voice. "We're having an early lunch on the terrace, and you have a visitor."

Dom and Isobel followed Aunt Eloise up to the house. Giles was already sitting at the table and next to him was a slightly nervous-looking Abi Watkins. "Hello, Dom. I was just passing when your Uncle Giles asked me to come to lunch," said Abi. "He practically kidnapped me," she added in a whisper to Dom as he sat down next to her.

Eloise began ladling leek soup into bowls. "How are you enjoying your stay, Dominic?" she asked. "I haven't seen nearly enough of you, and you are my only nephew. Where have you been? What have you been doing?"

Dom felt decidedly uneasy. "I'm having a super time, Aunt Eloise," he said vaguely. "Thank you so much for your invitation."

"But what have you been doing, child?" Aunt Eloise repeated.

Uncle Giles was about to join in the interrogation, when he suddenly reared back from the table, beads of sweat lining his forehead. "No, not again!" he moaned. It was though something horrifying was lunging at him out of the table itself! His knuckles had gone white. Aunt Eloise hurried over to him.

She steered the still ranting Uncle Giles in the direction of the house. "He needs a little rest. That's all," she called out. "It stresses him so to see his poor brother in such a bad state all the time."

"I've never heard either of them say a kind word about poor old Charles," said Isobel, the moment they were out of earshot.

They don't care about Charles.

"That's the second time I've seen my Uncle Giles do that," said Dom. "From what he said last time, I reckon he thinks he's being attacked by a dog."

"Imaginary terrors . . ." Isobel muttered.

"But those invisible birds that attacked *you* must have been real enough," Abi protested. "They even scratched your face."

"It's Mesmo the Magnificent," Isobel announced. "He's the reason why I lured you to Mask Manor, Dom. I know it's hard to believe, but all of these strange happenings are his doing."

"I thought Mesmo was dead," Dom protested.

"He is," nodded Isobel. "But his power lives on."

"You mean that a dead magician is trying to control what's going on around us," said Abi. "That's crazy."

High up in a tree, a tiny wren was listening to every word they said.

The Dubious Document

Isobel led Dom and Abi to the library at the heart of the manor. "I wanted you to come to Mask Manor, Dom, because Mesmo is trying to right a wrong," she explained. "From what I can gather, he can only control adults when they're being childish, but he can control a *real* child – you – to do *real* good. Now he's trying to save my daughter and your uncle through you."

Isobel clicked open a secret compartment in a desk and pulled out some papers. "Look at this," she said, pointing to a document.

With ~~this~~ this document I, Charles 'Muscle' Bound, being of ~~sad~~ sound mind, body, senses and memory ~~stake me workers~~ state my wishes.

In the event that accident, illness or ~~ace~~ act of God should leave me unable to continue running my estate (Mask Manor and Mask Playhouse) and/or my Company, the following steps are to be taken.

Giles 'Egg' Bound, my brother, shall run my Company, on my behalf, for up to one year or until my recovery, whichever is the sooner.
If I do not recover within the one year period, the entire Company as well as my estate, shall pass into his hands and legally become his property at 6.00pm on the following ~~dog~~ day.

For this to come into effect, Giles must ~~singe~~ sign this document at the given time, in the presence of my solicitor Ian Beagle in the library of Mask Manor.

Signed: *Charles Bound*.

Charles Bound

Witnessed by: *F. Simmley*

F. Simmley

Dom and Abi read the document with growing amazement. When had the accident with the sandbag happened? Surely Uncle Giles was set to inherit everything very soon.

"Tomorrow evening at six o'clock, to be precise," said Isobel. "Unless, of course, we can prove that this document is the fake I think it is. Dom's Aunt Eloise claims to have found it when cleaning in here one day!" Isobel snorted. "A likely story."

"Any idea who F. Simmley is, Mrs. Beauchamp?" Abi asked Isobel. She peered closely at the witness's signature. "Perhaps she can tell us something."

"Evidently she was the housekeeper here before Mildred came," said Isobel, returning the papers to their secret compartment in the desk. "Charles's lawyer, Mr. Beagle, tracked her down a while back. She claimed that this document was typed by Charles and is genuine."

"But why would Dom's uncle write such a thing?" puzzled Abi. "It's almost as if he *knew* that he would end up in a trance."

"There's something fishy going on here," said Dom. "I don't know what it is, but I do know Uncle Giles and Aunt Eloise are up to something."

As they left the library, a melancholic howl echoed around Mask Manor. "It's Charles," sighed Isobel. "Mesmo hypnotized him into thinking that he's a wolf. I'd better go to him."

AOOOOOOOOWL

The Book of Change

A huge task lay ahead for Isobel, Dom and Abi. Somehow, they would have to try to free Charles from his trance, prove the document was a fake by six o'clock the next evening, and then – hardest and strangest of all – try to bring Jenny Beauchamp back. Dom was stunned that Mesmo had really turned her into a bird . . . and petrified that this same Mesmo was now trying to control events through him.

Time was running out. If they were going to do something, it would have to be soon. Isobel agreed to go about her everyday work as usual, so as not to arouse suspicion with Eloise and Giles. Abi offered to go and ask her grandpa if he remembered F. Simmley and where they might find her. Dom was left alone to think. He began walking in the grounds. The distant clock chimed.

BONG! BONG! BONG! BONG! The bells counted out the hour. But something was wrong. They did not stop. BONG! five, BONG! six, BONG! seven . . . faster and faster, until they were chiming in time with Dom's pounding heart. He felt giddy. He felt weak. This was the now-familiar feeling of not being in control of his own mind.

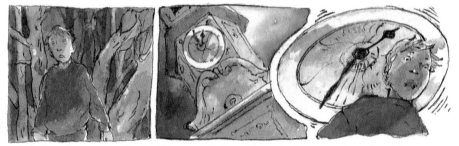

Although aware of what he was doing, Dom had no say in what his eyes showed him or where his feet took him. He was in the grip of Mesmo and drawn back inside the Playhouse. He climbed up onto the stage. Without hesitating, he lifted a trap door and went down some steps that he hadn't known were there. It was dark beneath the stage, but Dom made his way automatically to a door on the right.

The room beyond was windowless but not completely dark. A light pulsed from a crack between the doors of a wardrobe. Dom placed a chair by the wardrobe and – as he tugged open the doors with his clammy hands – a golden glow filled the room.

Bathed in the eerie light, Dom climbed onto the chair and reached up to the top shelf. His hands closed around an ancient book that seemed to pulsate with life. On the cover was its title: THE BOOK OF CHANGE and the symbol of a bird and fish. The four words seemed to burn deep inside his mind.

The same design!

At that moment, the light faded, the room was plunged into darkness and Dom was released from the grip of the trance. He fumbled through the blackness and out of the Playhouse. Back in daylight, he turned page after yellowed page of the ancient book. Apart from the title, it was written entirely in code.

It was hopeless. Obviously Dom was meant to find *The Book of Change*. But why, when he couldn't understand a single word of it?

Mesmo's Last Words

Dom managed to smuggle *The Book of Change* into Mask Manor, and up into his room, without being spotted by his Uncle Giles or Aunt Eloise. This avoided any awkward questions.

He sat on his bed in the Paisley Room, staring glumly at the coded writing. Where to start? Somewhere in the pages must lurk a vital clue . . . but what was it? Where was it?

Dom suddenly became aware of slight movement around him. The ghastly wallpaper was beginning to shimmer and spin. Dom groaned.

As though his arms were being controlled by the strings of some great puppet master, Dom found himself turning to the inside of the back cover of the book. There, he found a page torn from a diary, dated the day before Mesmo's accident. "Look!" he said to Isobel, who had slipped quietly in through the door.

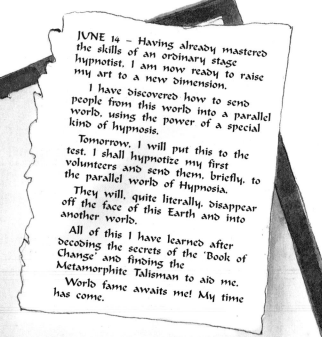

JUNE 14 – Having already mastered the skills of an ordinary stage hypnotist, I am now ready to raise my art to a new dimension.

I have discovered how to send people from this world into a parallel world, using the power of a special kind of hypnosis.

Tomorrow, I will put this to the test. I shall hypnotize my first volunteers and send them, briefly, to the parallel world of Hypnosia.

They will, quite literally, disappear off the face of this Earth and into another world.

All of this I have learned after decoding the secrets of the 'Book of Change' and finding the Metamorphite Talisman to aid me.

World fame awaits me! My time has come.

Isobel and Dom read the diary entry in stunned silence. As mad as it sounded, much of what Mesmo had written made sense. "So *that's* what Mesmo did to Jenny," said Isobel. "He seemed to turn her into a bird, but somehow sent her to the parallel world of Hypnosia . . . and she's been trapped there *a year to the day*! No wonder he sounded so guilty at the end."

"Sounded guilty?" Dom said in amazement. "But I thought Mesmo was killed by the sandbag?"

"Not at once," said Isobel. "The sandbag only knocked him out to begin with." She sighed. "When he first came around, Mesmo had total amnesia. He couldn't remember who he was or what he'd done to Jenny and Charles. He just stared up at us out of his hospital bed, with a childlike smile on his lips."

"How terrible," said Dom. "You must have felt so helpless."

Isobel nodded grimly. "Hours before he died, everything must have come back to him. He called out, 'The stage. The bird. It worked!' and then said Jenny's name again and again. After that, he lapsed into gibberish about a key."

She paused and stared into space, trying to remember Mesmo's exact words. "That was it. *The key linked to time that is upside-down and back-to-front.*' The poor man was raving."

An image suddenly flashed into Dom's mind . . . an image somehow linked to time. "I know what those words mean . . . " gasped Dom. "I'm sure of it. At least, I know that I have the answer locked away up here." He tapped his head. "If only I could unlock the memory!"

The Key to Time

Night came and went. Today was the day that Uncle Giles would inherit everything, unless he could be stopped. Dom hurried to the Watkins' cottage where he had arranged to meet Abi.

"Grandpa has some important news!" she said, throwing open the door. "It's about Miss Simmley who witnessed the document. She was Flora the housekeeper up at Mask Manor. Your uncle fired her years ago and . . ."

"Is your grandpa willing to help us to do whatever it is Mesmo wants us to do?" asked Dom. "It's obvious that he doesn't like anyone up at the Manor."

"Shh!" said Abi. "He has good reason to have bad feelings. Don't forget that it was Isobel Beauchamp who told the police that she saw Grandpa on the catwalk above the stage just before the sandbag fell . . . "

"Or was dropped, " added Larry Watkins appearing in a doorway. "That's what the police implied, based on the word of that one woman."

"I'm sure she only told them what she saw, Mr. Watkins," said Dom.

"And what about poor Simon Steele?" Abi's grandpa went on. "When he was playing Polonius, he was stabbed by your Uncle Charles playing Hamlet. The physical wound healed, but Steele was crippled by stagefright every time he went on stage after that. His career was at an end."

"But what else about Flora Simmley, Mr. Watkins?" Dom asked quickly.

Larry Watkins peered at Dom from the shadows. "Flora Simmley was on the catwalk with me that night. She'd left the village years before and had no business being there. She could easily have dropped that sandbag – deliberately. Who knows, she might even have been aiming it at your uncle. She certainly hated him after he fired her for stealing."

Dom was about to ask more when the dying words of Mesmo suddenly sprang to mind: *'the key linked to time that is upside-down and back-to-front'*. They were somehow connected to this very house. That was it! Dom dashed over to a strange old watch with unusual numbers. He remembered now. He had seen it among the theatrical props during his last visit.

"This is it!" said Dom, clutching the watch excitedly. "This watch has numbers that are *'upside-down and back-to-front.'* This must somehow be linked to the *The Book of Change*." Abi and her grandpa looked at him blankly. Of course, Dom hadn't even had time to tell Abi about *The Book of Change*. No wonder she looked so confused.

"It is a beautiful timepiece," said Mr. Watkins. "Mavis found it in the Playhouse after the doomed variety show. No one has ever claimed it."

Dom was stunned. Surely they must know whose watch it was? "It belonged to Mesmo," he told them.

"I was having trouble with a faulty spotlight for much of that evening," said Abi's grandfather. "I didn't have a chance to see Mesmo at work. Abi was in bed with flu. No wonder the watch was never claimed . . ."

Dom studied the magician's prop. On the other end of its chain was a blue disk with the – now familiar – fish and bird symbol in the middle. Was this somehow *'the key linked to time that is upside-down and back-to-front'* ?

Just then, the back of the watch sprang open, and a square of folded paper fluttered out. It was covered in letters and symbols. Of course! Dom thought. The full meaning of the magician's message had fallen into place. The *key* was the key to the code in *The Book of Change*. With it, he should be able to decode the book and find a way of helping Uncle Charles and Jenny.

"May I borrow this watch?" he asked Abi's grandpa, who nodded. "Thanks," said Dom. "Uncle Charles could have a great deal to thank you for, Mr. Watkins."

Unwelcome Visitors

On the way back to Mask Manor, Dom told Abi how he'd been led to *The Book of Change* and about Mesmo's last words to Isobel. Once back in his room, he showed Abi Mesmo's diary entry. Now they must decode the book using the key written on the piece of paper that had fallen from the watch.

But where should they start? At six o'clock Uncle Charles would lose everything . . . and it could take days to find a part in the book that might explain how to bring him out of his trance. The task seemed impossible.

Then something happened that stunned them both. With the key to the code in one hand and the book in the other, Abi made an extraordinary discovery. The coded symbols on certain pages or passages of the book became ordinary words before her eyes. She could read them as easily as if they were written in English, even if the language itself seemed awkward and ancient. "Mesmo must be channelling some of his power through me!" she gasped. "Quickly, Dom. Write this part down." With that, Abi read out a passage from the book which Dom wrote onto a notepad.

Metamorphite is the rarest and greatest of all rocks in this, our humble, world – for this is not the only world as you shall learn. There is but one place to find this Metamorphite and that is in the flatlands where once there were the mighty Cocoon Mountains.

Here, for over 2 million summers, giant butterflies ruled the valleys and the mountain tops, but then their reign ended and they ceased to be. Century after century passed and the butterfly wings became pressed together to form the thinnest layer of that which we now call Metamorphite.

The largest piece of Metamorphite became the all-powerful Metamorphite Talisman, a disk small enough to hold in the palm of thy hand but, with the right incantations, powerful enough to transport you,. hypnotized, to Hypnosia – a world in a parallel dimension.

"Wow!" said Dom when he'd finished writing down the passage Abi had just read out to him. "The fish and bird disk on Mesmo's watch must be the Metamorphite Talisman. He must have used it and some of the incantations from this book in the variety show . . . and sent Jenny to the parallel world."

"What *are* incantations?" asked Abi, studying the book even more closely.

"I'm not sure," said Dom. "They're spells or special chants, I think."

Abi flipped through the ancient pages, frantically trying to find anything that might be an incantation. Her eyes came to rest on a particular paragraph of symbols that read like words to her.

"Listen to this," she said. "It says that for a person to pass from our world into Hypnosia or from Hypnosia to our world they must '*change into an animal form other than their own, whether it be beast, fish or fowl.*' " Her face dropped. "It also says that '*Though not an impossibility to travel between the two worlds without the Talisman, to do so would be a danger to all.*' "

Abi was interrupted by a sudden loud tapping. Dom knew, with a shudder, that the birds were back. He turned in horror. This time, they were inside a mirror – on the other side – beaks and claws scraping and tapping the glass.

Messages

"There's still so much I don't understand!" cried Dom. "Are these birds visitors from the parallel world? If so, what do they want from us?"

"L–Look," said Abi, pointing to a page she had just turned to in *The Book of Change*. "Pictures . . . and they're moving." As Abi and Dom stared at the book, a story unfolded before their very eyes . . .

"Who'd want to be in a trance all the time?" asked Abi. "It must be like being a zombie or something. No fun. This parallel universe sounds scary too. Imagine being hypnotized to another dimension . . . It's incredible!"

"And dangerous," Dom added.

"Dangerous?" demanded Aunt Eloise bursting into the room. "What's dangerous?"

"Nothing, Aunt Eloise," said Dom, in utter amazement.

"I'll give you *nothing*," she snarled. "From tonight, things are going to be very different at Mask Manor. Just you wait and see!" Her eyes fell on Abi. "You. Here again?" she shouted, her voice trembling with rage. She waved a typed letter at them. "If I find either of you had anything to do with this . . . this . . . " Too angry to speak, she ripped the letter to pieces, stuffed the pieces into her pocket, and stormed out of the room.

EE YOU THEN.

LES.

A single fragment fell from her pocket to the floor. Dom managed to hide it under his elbow before Aunt Eloise turned around and gave one final menacing glare through the doorway. As she disappeared down the corridor, Dom heard her mutter: "Soon all this shall be mine."

Out of Thin Air

Time flew by, with Abi reading out decoded passages from *The Book of Change*, and Dom writing them down. At last – fingers firmly crossed – they thought that they might just have enough to bring Uncle Charles out of his trance and Jenny Beauchamp back from Hypnosia.

The major problem was that, according to the book, the special incantations would have to be read out at the very place where the damage had first been done. That would mean a trip to the Mask Playhouse as soon as possible.

Luck was on their side when they heard a car in the driveway. Dashing outside, Dom and Abi found Isobel about to take Charles for his usual late afternoon drive, as if it were just another ordinary day.

"Quick, Mrs. Beauchamp," said Dom, jumping into the back seat with Abi. "We must get to the Playhouse as fast as possible. We think we have all we need from *The Book of Change*."

As Isobel sped down the winding country lanes to the Playhouse, Dom quickly outlined what he and Abi had managed to glean from the incredible book.

"If we want to be in with a chance of freeing Uncle Charles from his trance and stopping Uncle Giles and Aunt Eloise getting their hands on everything, we're going to have to work fast," he said.

Arriving at the Playhouse, Abi and Dom rushed ahead with the decoded *Book of Change* and the disk that was the Metamorphite Talisman. Isobel followed close behind, guiding the entranced Charles Bound onto the stage. Moments later, talisman raised, Abi began reading the first incantation . . .

'The power of the butterfly wings be here
The path between opposite worlds appear.
Where tomorrow's dreams will now abide;
Where the body shall be, the mind will reside.
With this key I unlock the doors . . .
. . . RETURN!'

The Metamorphite Talisman had begun to glow and pulsate as the words
were spoken. On the word *'RETURN'*, it flashed a brilliant blue and poured a
stream of light straight into Charles's eyes. Dom's uncle jumped as if a bolt of
electricity had shot through his body.

Charles Bound stared around in wonderment. When he saw Isobel, his face
broke into a smile. "It worked! Thanks to you all, it worked. Now we must get
Jenny back. That's more important than anything," he said, stretching. "I've
been trapped *between* the two parallel worlds, with my mind seeing and
hearing everything, but my body unable to react or respond," he said. "But
Jenny is in Hypnosia itself. She keeps trying to come back to you, in the form
of a wren, and if we leave it much longer, she may be unable to return at all."

Dom put his fingers to his lips as Abi, for a second time, raised her right
arm. This time she recited a slightly different incantation. Nothing happened.
Her words echoed emptily around the Mask Playhouse. Jenny did not appear.

Metamorphosis

The silence was finally broken by Dom. "Don't give up hope, Mrs. Beauchamp," he told Isobel. "There might be another way to bring Jenny back. There is a passage in *The Book of Change* called '*The power of metamorphosis*' . . . "

"That would mean one of us changing into another kind of animal and bringing Jenny back!" cried Uncle Charles, rubbing his eyes. "I think that should be me."

"No, uncle," said Dom gravely. "I have Mesmo's guiding force to help me. I must undergo the metamorphosis."

"Good luck," said Abi. With the talisman held high, and a new incantation passing from her lips, she hypnotized Dom – and the impossible happened.

He turned into a peregrine falcon. In this new and powerful form, Dom flew up and disappeared into the middle of the Metamorphite Talisman's glowing light. He felt a slight breeze ruffle his feathers as he flew through time and space . . . into the parallel world of Hypnosia.

Time passed slowly for Abi, Isobel and Charles waiting on the empty stage. Abi was beginning to get desperate when, suddenly, there was a flurry of wings. It was Dom, still in the form of the peregrine falcon – and in his talons was a wren!

But the peregrine and the wren were not the only birds to appear. One after the other they came. A magpie, a crow, an owl . . . more and more and more . . . swooping, screeching, diving . . .

"The gate between us and Hypnosia must be closed forever," cried Abi. "According to the book, it is too late for these descendants of the Lantisians to return to human form. They could upset the balance of Nature itself." Abi raised both her arms and recited a final incantation from *The Book of Change*. The birds turned tail and vanished, leaving only their plaintive cries.

At the same moment, the bodies of the peregrine falcon and the wren began to ripple and writhe. They grew and contorted until they had returned to the human forms of Dom and Jenny.

"Welcome home!" cried Isobel, running over to her daughter. Jenny looked a year older but, otherwise, unchanged by her terrifying ordeal.

Uncle Charles shook Dom firmly by the hand. "What you and Abi have been through to help us is more than anyone could ever ask. Thank you."

"What about my friends?" asked Jenny. "What about the Lantisians who came here with me from Hypnosia as birds . . . and risked so much to try to make you help me?"

Uncle Charles put his hand on her shoulder. "We'll never forget their part in returning you to this world, Jenny," he said quietly. "But they are destined to stay in Hypnosia forever. Like Mesmo, their ancestors were dabbling in something they did not understand . . . and that can be a very dangerous thing to do."

"The document!" cried Dom, suddenly remembering the time. "We must stop the signing back at Mask Manor!"

"Yes!" cried Charles. "It's time for the final showdown!"

To Mask Manor!

Masks Off

After a hair-raising drive, the five of them arrived at Mask Manor. They sprinted to the library with pounding hearts. As Charles burst in, Eloise, Giles and a man that Dom assumed to be the lawyer looked around. The three of them were standing by the desk, where the document lay. Giles had a pen in his hand. "SIGN IT!" Eloise screeched, but Giles seemed frozen in position.

STOP!

Charles strode across the room, seized the fake document and tore it up. "I don't think we'll be needing this," he said. Ian Beagle – Charles's lawyer – looked dumbfounded but delighted by his client's remarkable recovery.

Next to him, Giles was cowering in fear. Charles laughed. "It looks as if Mesmo has been conjuring up another vision of ghosts and ghouls to try to stop the signing of this pack of lies," he said. "Oh yes. I know exactly what's been going on. I may not have been able to react when in my trance, but I've seen and heard everything. Perfectly." Giles stared miserably at the carpet as Charles turned to him calmly. "I see you're suffering a different kind of fear to the stagefright you used to suffer, *Simon Steele*," he said.

Dom gasped. Simon Steele? This wasn't his Uncle Giles at all. It was the actor, Simon Steele, impersonating him. The man who had been stabbed by Uncle Charles in *Hamlet*. That explained it. There had been something bothering Dom from the beginning. Giles was supposed to be hairless, but Dom had seen a razor and shaving brush in his room – Steele must have had to shave his head every day to look the part.

"So where's the *real* Giles Bound?" asked Abi.

Charles shrugged. "Who knows. Fifteen years ago he rejected the material world and set off with his few remaining possessions on his back." He turned to the woman Dom knew as Aunt Eloise. "I see that you decided to dye your hair," he said. "You must have been so frustrated when the sandbag you aimed at me hit poor old Mesmo instead, *Flora Simmley.* "

Dom, Abi and Isobel were flabbergasted. This was the F. Simmley who had 'witnessed' the forged document. This was the woman who had been on the catwalk above the stage the night the sandbag fell. This was the F. S. whose initials appeared on one of the paintings in the studio upstairs. "Pah!" she snorted. "It took years of planning. It would have worked too . . . "

"If Mesmo hadn't reached out from across the grave and used his powers to make things right – with more than a little help from my nephew Dominic, and Abi Watkins too," grinned Charles.

Just then, a violent rumbling thundered through the entire manor. It was as if an earthquake had seized the building and was shaking it to its very foundations.

Everyone grabbed the nearest piece of furniture. "What NOW?" yelled Dom.

Out of the Ashes

Dom looked around the library, terrified, as leatherbound books crashed to the floor and windows rattled in their frames. If this carried on much longer, Mask Manor would soon end up a heap of rubble. Suddenly, he had a flash of inspiration. "Abi! Let go of the talisman!" he bellowed.

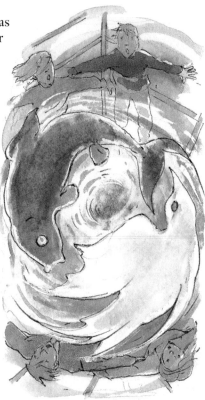

Abi did as she was told. The Metamorphite Talisman soared into the air, Mesmo's watch still dangling from the other end of the chain. It hovered in midair but the deafening rumbling continued.

"And *The Book of Change*!" Dom added urgently. The heavy volume flew up and began revolving around the talisman. At the same time, everyone found themselves thrown back against the shelving that lined the walls. They stared at the two objects which suddenly burst into blue and purple flames that spun around and around . . . in the forms of a bird and a fish, like the symbol on the talisman.

Then, as abruptly as they had appeared, the swirling flames vanished. A dusting of ash fell to the carpet. The atmosphere immediately became cheerier, lighter – as if a great burden had been lifted. Dom and Abi somehow sensed that Mesmo had departed. Having righted the wrongs he had done *and* made sure that no one could ever repeat his mistakes, he had found peace.

With Charles Bound back in charge, Mask Manor was swiftly returned to its former glory. The tennis lawns were mowed and marked, the swimming pool was cleaned out and even the fearful Paisley Room wallpaper was covered with a thick layer of paint.

The mysterious dropped fragment from the letter soon fell into place too. The 'LES' at the bottom had been the last three letters of a name – none other than that of the real Giles. After years of silence, he was returning to Mask Manor with amazing news. Even Charles didn't recognize him when he arrived. He had thick hair and a thick beard.

"It was incredible, Charlie," he said. "I met a hermit who sold me a miracle hair tonic. He said that it came from a place called the lost city of Lantisia and – "

"Enough!" Charles exclaimed theatrically. "I never want to hear the names Lantisia or Hypnosia ever again."

Dom grinned. He couldn't agree more. These things belonged to the past, like the Paisley Room's appalling wallpaper.

The Mask Playhouse was soon back in use too. Its first production wasn't a production of *Hamlet*, nor a variety show. It was a unique performance – the wedding of Charles and Isobel.

The fake Uncle Giles and Aunt Eloise – Simon Steele and Flora Simmley – regretted that they were unable to attend. They regretted many things. They were behind prison bars. To everyone's obvious relief, there was someone else who did not put in an unbilled appearance either. Mesmo the Magnificent, of course.

Did You Spot?

You can use this page to help spot things that could be useful in solving the mystery. First, there are hints and clues you can read as you go along. They will give you some idea of what to look out for. Then there are extra notes to read which tell you more about what happened afterwards.

Hints and Clues

51   Invisible birds? There's more to them than meets the eye!

52-53   Study these people with care. You never know when and where they might pop up again in the story.

54-55   Keep your eyes peeled. Everyday objects could be important clues.

56-57   Dom is experiencing odd things when awake and asleep. The nightmare could be important.

58-59   Read the newspaper clipping with care.

60-61   Study the cottage, both inside and out.

62-63   The species of birds might be vital later.

64-65   Another bird – and a bird and fish symbol on the disk, too. What can the strange symbol mean?

66-67   Look at the paintings closely. They hold more than one clue.

68-69   Familiarize yourself with these key events and *people* in the Mask Playhouse's past.

70-71   A safe full of money? Aren't the Bounds supposed to be hard up?

72-73   Jenny became a wren? That explains a great deal. Think back.

74-75   What other events could Mesmo have been controlling?

76-77   The document is appallingly typed. Who mentioned their typing earlier? Hmm.

78-79   It's the bird and fish symbol again. This book must be important.

80-81   Time . . . *upside-down and back-to-front*. There has been something that fits the bill. What was it?

82-83   Flora Simmley's initials have appeared somewhere earlier.

84-85   So Mesmo can extend his power to controlling Abi, another child.

86-87   Who is 'LES'? Or could it be the end of a name?

88-89   '*The power of the butterfly wings*' refers to the Metamorphite.

90-91   Things should begin to fall into place by now.

In the End

Simon Steele finally lost his stage fright. In prison, he took the lead role in Harry Pinta's play *A Boring Bloke*. Seven prisoners escaped during the first performance.

By the Way . . .

Flora Simmley was so busy watching the stage on the night she dropped the sandbag, that she didn't see who Charles was with in the audience. This was lucky for Isobel, whose 'nurse' story might have been questioned if Flora had recognized her from the Playhouse.

When in the role of 'Aunt Eloise', Flora was careful to avoid those who might have known her in the past – including Abi's grandpa, Larry Watkins. She often only went out after dark.

Did you spot?

Mesmo's face appears a number of times in Mask Manor – even peering out of a painting by 'Aunt Eloise'. See if you can see where else he is lurking.

Dom chose to become a Peregrine Falcon because it's one of the fastest birds in the world.

Nightmare at Mystery Mansion

Phil Roxbee Cox

Illustrated by Sue Hellard

Designed by Lindy Dark

Edited by
Michelle Bates

Contents

The Nightmare Begins

On the stroke of midnight, a scream rang out from the depths of Mystery Mansion. The eerie sound seemed to fill the still night air. It crossed the dank and lifeless marshlands and reached the ears of a lone figure in the churchyard of St. Judas.

James Flint, the old grave digger, shuddered at the unholy scream, but did not cease from his task. This wasn't the first strange noise to come from Mystery Mansion, and he didn't suppose it would be the last. He mopped his sweating brow with a large, ragged handkerchief, then tossed another spadeful of soil over his shoulder. There were still two more graves to be dug that night . . .

A noise, much closer this time, caused Flint to look up with a start. He thought he saw two eyes staring at him from the silhouette of a yew tree.

"Who's there?" he demanded. He tried to sound confident, but the scream had unsettled him and his voice squeaked with fear.

Then he saw the animal, staring down at him in the space he had dug for a coffin. At first, the grave digger thought that it was an enormous hound. Then he realized that it was a wolf. And not just any wolf. It was the wolf that had stalked his dreams for over sixty years.

A second scream filled the air. This time, it came from the churchyard. This time, it was the very human scream of James Flint himself.

Below Stairs

Life was hard for the servants at Mystery Mansion. So hard, that they called it *Misery* Mansion, but not in front of Mr. Paulfrey. Mr. Paulfrey was the head butler and the most important servant in the house.

There were twenty-eight servants at Mystery Mansion and, according to Mr. Paulfrey, Harry Grubb was the least important of them all. Harry was the boot boy and, like all the other servants, lived in fear of Mr. Paulfrey.

You're the lowest of the low, Grubb.

Harry's job of cleaning all the boots and shoes not only kept him tired and dirty, but also kept him 'below stairs'. This meant that he wasn't allowed into the rooms occupied by Lord Rakenhell, the master of Mystery Mansion, or those of his family.

There was only one person that the servants feared more than Mr. Paulfrey, and that was his Lordship. Though few servants had ever met Lord Rakenhell face-to-face, all had heard his cries of rage.

In fact, there were only two people Harry Grubb liked in the whole house. One was Anna, a dusting duty maid, and the other was Miss Charlotte, Lord Rakenhell's only daughter. In the case of Miss Charlotte, he only liked her from a distance. He had never actually *spoken* to her.

All that was to change one December morning. Harry had been instructed by the cook to take a message to Tom Liddle, the gamekeeper, who lived in a cottage on the other side of the estate. It was bitterly cold, so Harry decided to run there to keep warm. The cold air stung his reddened cheeks. Thick frost crunched beneath his feet, and rows of icicles hung from many of the trees he dashed past.

As he came to the edge of a rose garden, he saw smoke from a bonfire coiling up into the crisp morning air like a charmed snake leaving its basket. He stopped to warm himself in front of the crackling flames and thought of the fireplace in the attic room of Mystery Mansion that he shared with three other boys. They were only given one piece of coal to burn each night. He shuddered. How he *hated* Mystery Mansion.

Harry's thoughts were interrupted by a voice barking: "It's Grubb, isn't it?" Harry looked up to see Mr. Colly, the head gardener, staring at him.

"Yes, Mr. Colly," he replied.

"What are you doing here? Shouldn't you be working back at the house?" the gardener asked. Harry told him about the message he had to deliver to Tom Liddle, the gamekeeper.

"Then you can do something for me too," said Mr. Colly. "Instead of crossing the river at Ford's Bridge to reach Liddle's cottage, cross it farther down where the old tree has fallen across it. Do you know where I mean?" Harry nodded, watching the gardener's words turn to steam as they left his mouth and came into contact with the cold air.

"Good. Well, when you've crossed the river, you'll see an old hollow tree just off to your right. I want you to put a parcel in the trunk of the tree." Colly rummaged around in a wheelbarrow and produced a parcel wrapped in brown paper.

Tell no one.
Is that understood?
No one.

"Yes, Mr. Colly," said Harry. He tucked the parcel under his arm and set off at a sprint. The new route would take him longer, and he didn't want Cook complaining that he'd deliberately taken his time to get out of doing other work.

He hurried through the fields until, up ahead, he could see the tree which had fallen across the river the summer-before-last. Then he heard a voice. It was coming from the river. It was a girl's voice crying out for help.

101

To the Rescue

Harry dashed over to the riverbank and looked over the edge. Instead of flowing water, he was faced by a sheet of ice. The river had frozen over!

The ice looked thick, but obviously not thick enough to support the weight of a child for, to his left, he could see that Charlotte Rakenhell had fallen through the ice and was now up to her shoulders in freezing water.

"Help me! Please help me!" she wailed. Harry rushed over to the fallen tree and broke off one of the branches. Dragging it across the ground, he swung one end over the river bank to within the girl's reach.

"Grab the end of this, Miss Charlotte," he shouted. "I'll pull you out." Lord Rakenhell's frightened daughter clutched her end of the branch, and Harry pulled with all his might. He heard her yelp with pain as she rubbed against the jagged ice and was pulled up the bank to safety.

Charlotte lay on the ground gasping for breath and shivering. On her feet were a pair of ice skates. "You must get out of your wet clothes before you catch your death of cold, Miss Charlotte," said Harry.

Charlotte's eyes widened. "What would I change into?" she asked, her teeth chattering like clattering knitting needles.

"At least take off your coat and wear this," Harry urged. Slipping off his old jacket, he held it out to her. Without a word, she did as he suggested.

Harry knew he must get her back to the house to dry out and warm up. "Take off your skates, Miss," he said, hurrying over to where she'd left her winter boots. He brought them to Charlotte and helped her put them on.

They ran across the fields toward Mystery Mansion. Charlotte was shivering so much now that Harry changed his plan and led her to Mr. Colly's bonfire.

"Warm yourself as best you can, miss," he said. "I'll see if I can find you some more dry clothes." Harry went into the potting shed and found a pair of gardening gloves, a smock and a battered hat. Fortunately, Mr. Colly was nowhere to be seen. Charlotte went into the shed and came out dressed in the dry clothes. Harry couldn't help smiling when he saw her. She looked like a scarecrow.

"What are you laughing at – ?" she began. Then, as the warmth started to return to her bones, she smiled. "I suppose I must look rather silly. What's your name? I've seen you up at the house." Harry told her. "Well, thank you for saving me, Harry, but it must be our secret. My father would be very angry if he knew that I'd been skating on my own. He'd be even more angry if he heard I'd had an accident. You must promise to tell no one," she ordered.

"I promise, miss," said Harry. "But, if you'll forgive me asking, how will you explain your clothes?"

"If anyone asks, I shall say that I have been dressing up. I am a Rakenhell, so no one will dare argue with me. Please take my wet clothes to the laundry room for me," she said, handing them to him.

As Harry took the bundle from her, his heart sank. It reminded him of the package Mr. Colly had given him. He must have dropped it by the river bank when he had rescued Miss Charlotte! And he still hadn't delivered Cook's message to the gamekeeper. He would be in big trouble.

103

From Bad to Worse

Harry hunted high and low for the package, but without success. In the end, he gave up looking and delivered Cook's message to the gamekeeper. He then returned to Mystery Mansion. Slipping into the laundry room, he hid Miss Charlotte's wet things in among some other clothes.

As he tiptoed into the corridor, he walked bang into Mr. Paulfrey. "What have you been doing?" the butler snarled.

"I've just been delivering a message to Tom Liddle for Cook, Mr. P–P–Paulfrey," Harry stammered.

"You should have been back over an hour ago, boy," said the butler. "I think you've been hiding in the nice warm laundry room instead of working. You shall have to be punished. Are you afraid of good, honest hard work and a little cold weather?"

"N–No, sir," said Harry, thinking that, if life were fair, he would have been hailed a hero for saving Miss Charlotte's life. Instead, he was facing punishment.

Punishments for servants at Mystery Mansion had to be carefully planned. There was no point in locking someone in his or her room because it would probably be more fun than working! Sometimes, servants who had angered Mr. Paulfrey went without food. Once a maid had been made to eat a lump of coal for stealing a bread roll.

Harry Grubb's punishment was very simple. He had to clean all the boots and shoes that he would have had to clean anyway – only he had to do it outside in the freezing cold. The scullery maids were under strict instructions to make sure that he didn't come inside until the very last shoe was polished. They all felt sorry for Harry – especially Anna – but, at the same time, none of them dared disobey Mr. Paulfrey.

After a while, Harry began shivering as much as Charlotte had been when he had rescued her. His body was covered in goose bumps, and his fingers were stiff with cold. He couldn't hold the shoebrush properly and he felt like crying.

"Harry!" a voice called out. The boot boy looked around the courtyard, but couldn't see anyone. "Harry!" the voice called again. This time he spotted Charlotte at a window. She was wearing a thick purple dress and looked none the worse for her icy swim. "What's going on?"

When Harry had finished explaining, Charlotte looked outraged. "Well, I am ordering you to go back inside, and tell Cook to give you some warm soup," she said. "Is that clear?"

"Y-Y-Yes, miss," said Harry. Nothing like this had ever happened at Mystery Mansion before.

At first, Cook couldn't believe her ears when Harry shuffled into the kitchen and explained that he'd been ordered to ask for soup. But soon she realized that he wouldn't dare make up such a story, and poured him a steaming bowlful.

When the news reached Mr. Paulfrey, he was furious and he stormed into the kitchen. "I expect you're feeling very pleased with yourself, Grubb," he said. "But remember this – Miss Rakenhell took pity on you this afternoon, but has probably forgotten you already. I, on the other hand, will not forget . . . and *I* see you every day. Back to work!"

In the warmth of the boot room, Harry set about his tasks when a figure appeared in the doorway. It was Mr. Colly. "You didn't deliver my package!" he whispered. "What have you done with it?" Harry groaned. How he hated Mystery Mansion.

The Church of St. Judas

The following day, there were four burials in the churchyard of St. Judas. Three of these were for men who had strayed from one of the paths through the misty marshland and had sunk in boggy ground.

The marshland around Mystery Mansion seemed to be governed by its own rules of nature. Paths that were safe one week became dangerous the next. Few local people dared to cross the marsh, with its strange mists and eerie yellow night-time glow.

The fourth funeral was for James Flint, the grave digger. He had rushed home in the middle of the night, screaming something about 'wolves', and died, exhausted, in his bed. This hadn't surprised many villagers. Most of them had thought that old Jimmy Flint had been strange all his life.

As the last of the mourners left the last of the funerals, Magnus Duggan, the clock winder, went inside the church of St. Judas. These last few nights he'd been sleeping badly. Noises kept on waking him . . . noises that came from the heart of Mystery Mansion.

When Duggan wasn't being kept awake at night, he was having nightmares – usually the *same* nightmare, over and over again. As he put away the hymn books, he thought he heard a scuffling noise coming from somewhere in the bell tower.

A few weeks before, he had found the local vagabond, Struan Maggot, fast asleep at the back of the church. A storm had been raging outside, and it was a warm, dry place to be. The clock winder couldn't really blame Struan for being there. However, if the vagabond was sleeping in the church again, Duggan would have to have stern words with him.

The clock winder strode across the cold stone floor and threw open the door. "Who's there?" he called. There was no reply. Although it was still daylight outside, the spiral staircase inside the bell tower was dark and forbidding. There were no lights inside the tower.

Magnus Duggan began walking slowly up the stairs. "Is there anybody there?" he asked. He listened and, above the pounding of his own heart, he heard a definite scuffling up ahead.

H-Hello?

This was ridiculous. He had been clock winder at St. Judas for many years, and had never felt in the slightest bit scared before. It was those awful nightmares, that were making him feel so uneasy now . . .

Suddenly, a moving shadowy mass seemed to appear from nowhere, and surround him. Magnus Duggan screamed. He saw bats. Hundreds of them. He screamed again and fell back down the stairs . . . just as he had in his nightmares.

A Place to Hide

Three weeks passed, the weather worsened and Harry the boot boy didn't hear any more from Mr. Colly about the undelivered package. Perhaps Mr. Colly had searched along the riverbank and found it himself? Harry didn't think it very likely. But one thing seemed clear. Mr. Colly didn't want anyone to know about the errand.

That made two secrets he had to keep. He was bursting to tell Anna, the maid, about saving Miss Charlotte's life. But he had kept his promise to Lord Rakenhell's daughter, and said nothing.

Christmas drew nearer. Not that Christmas was a festive time for the servants at Mystery Mansion. At this time of year, they didn't call it *Misery* Mansion but *Miserly* Mansion. No one was given any time off. They had no fun and no parties. Mr. Paulfrey and a reluctant Mrs. Weatherspoon, the housekeeper, were the only ones to have a special Christmas meal.

Every year, Mr. Paulfrey gave instructions that any leftovers from the enormous feast, which Lord Rakenhell enjoyed with his family, should be fed to the dogs. Not so much as a mingy morsel should pass the other servants' lips.

It was the week before Christmas when Charlotte Rakenhell and Harry Grubb spoke to each other again. Charlotte was having a party with the children of other rich landowners in the district. There were well-fed children in expensive clothes running all over Mystery Mansion.

Not all of the children who had been invited had come, however. Some parents had heard stories of the strange noises coming from the house, and didn't want them visiting it.

> You're not going there, Arabella. It's a bad place.

Charlotte wanted to play a kind of hide-and-seek where everyone ends up hiding in the same place. She wanted to be the first person to hide and needed a really good hiding place. Who better to ask than a servant, who used parts of the house she had never been in? Everyone would be hunting for her for hours. She went to the boot room and found Harry hard at work as always.

"Don't you get bored doing that all day?" she asked.

Harry looked up in surprise. "No, Miss Charlotte," he said. "I mean, it's the only thing I know how to do. Who knows, one day I might be a butler like Mr. Paulfrey."

"A butler, perhaps, Harry, but not like Paulfrey I hope. He's such a horrid man. I don't know why Papa puts up with him,"

Charlotte sighed. Then she told him about needing a good hiding place.

Harry knew such a place. There was a big storage cupboard that wasn't used any more, down at the end of the corridor joining the servants' quarters to the main part of the house. The door to the cupboard was hidden behind an old tapestry. Unless you knew it was there, it would take ages to find it.

"Come on, Miss Charlotte. I'll show you," he said. He led her down the corridor and pulled back the tapestry. "Here," he said, triumphantly.

"You expect me and all my friends to be able to hide behind one mangy old tapestry?" she laughed. "We're not that thin."

"No. There's a storage cupboard here . . ." he began, turning to point out the hidden door. Only there was no door to be seen, just a blank wall. The door had disappeared.

Bump in the Night

That night, Harry's dreams were filled with terrible images of the evil Mr. Paulfrey. He woke with a start to find Anna shaking his shoulder. She wasn't allowed in this part of the house. They would both be in *big* trouble if she had been seen. Without waking the other boys in the room, they tiptoed out into the passageway.

"What is it?" he whispered.

"There are some strange new noises downstairs," Anna whispered back. "Different from the usual moaning and wailing."

All that Harry could hear was snoring coming from the other servants' bedrooms. "I don't hear anything," he said.

"I didn't say you could hear them from up here," she said. "I went downstairs to look for that silver locket my mother gave me. I lost it this afternoon and wanted to see if I could find it before we started work in the morning. Then I heard the noises. They're coming from under the floor. Come on."

Before Harry could stop her, Anna was creeping down the servants' stairs. Neither Mr. Paulfrey nor Mrs. Weatherspoon would take kindly to them wandering around at night. It was strictly against the rules.

When they reached the kitchen, Harry wanted to turn back. The servants often heard strange cries at night, but Mr. Paulfrey's instructions were clear. No one was even to mention them.

They entered the kitchen just as a loud groaning noise came from beneath the floor. It sounded like a wounded animal. Harry wished that he was back in his hard bed in the cold attic room.

"It's not like any of the other weird noises I've heard lately," whispered Anna. "It sounds almost human."

Harry took a candle from a shelf, lighting it from the one Anna was holding. A cockroach appeared from under a table and scurried over his bare feet. He shuddered. Harry held out his candle and looked at the floor to see if there were any other insects patrolling the huge flagstones under cover of darkness. His eyes were caught by the movement of one of the flagstones to

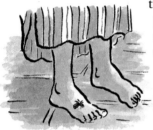

the right of him. Grabbing Anna, he pulled her around to the other side of the kitchen table. She blew out both of the candles.

Moments later, a new light shone out. A man was coming out from under the flagstone, lantern in hand. It must be a secret trap door. The stranger held the lantern high as a second person emerged from the trap door. It was none other than Mrs. Weatherspoon.

"Oh, I'll make him talk, don't you worry," the man told her.

A groan sounded from beneath the floor once more . . . a very human groan. The hairs on the back of Harry's neck stood up. He shuddered.

He'll talk. Give me time.

Unease in the Village

That same night, across the marshes at *The Bogside Inn*, the villager Thora Mulch was doing what she did best. Gossiping. If there was anything worth knowing in the village, she was the first to find it out. It was she who pointed out that local folk were having terrible nightmares and that some of their bad dreams were coming true.

"Old Jimmy Flint was haunted by the dreams of a wolf, but how many of you know that he had scratch marks on his face when he died?" she asked a group of men. The landlord of *The Bogside Inn* put the tankard he was polishing on the counter.

"The scratches could have been made by thorns, Thora. The churchyard at St. Judas is overgrown in parts," he reasoned. "And, from what I hear, real, live wolves are harmless beasts anyhow."

"Thorns?" scoffed Thora Mulch. "Harmless? They say that the scratches were like deep, deep, claw marks. And what about poor Mr. Duggan? He's been clock winder for I don't know how long. He must have been up and down those steps in the bell tower a thousand times. Only now he starts having nightmares about bats and suddenly he's attacked by a whole swarm of them. He's lucky he didn't break his neck, falling down them stairs."

"How is he now?" asked a man who was leaning on the bar, a tankard of foaming ale in his hand.

"Disappeared, that's how he is," said Thora Mulch. "The last anyone saw of him, he was in bed with a sore back and a bandage on his head. Now he's disappeared into thin air. This isn't the first disappearance. Mark my words, it has something to do with the big house. It ain't called *Mystery* Mansion for nothing."

The landlord laughed. "You're not talking to a bunch of outsiders now, Thora," he said. "We all know how Mystery Mansion got its name."

The village gossip snorted indignantly. "So you believe it was called *Misty* Mansion when it was built, do you?" she demanded.

"Of course I do," said the landlord. "It makes perfect sense to call the place Misty Mansion. It's always surrounded by mist from the marshlands. That filthy marsh gas is everywhere. Its name just changed over the years. It's as simple as that."

"The Rakenhells must have been crazy to build their home here," said Thora, eager to steer the conversation back to the strange happenings. "*Misty* or *Mystery*, there's something mighty odd happening in these parts."

Across the eerie, glowing marshland, Mystery Mansion rose out of the mist. Here, Harry and Anna's nightmares had only just begun.

There's evil in that house across the marshes.

Ruins by Moonlight

Back at the mansion, Harry and Anna remained crouched in the darkness long after Mrs. Weatherspoon and the stranger had shut the trap door and left the kitchen.

Harry's brain was reeling – trying to make sense of the extraordinary events they had just witnessed. What had the stranger said? *I'll make him talk*. Who talk? Who else was down there . . . and why wouldn't he talk? Harry had visions of someone being held prisoner in a secret cellar beneath the kitchen. Someone who was being tortured to tell some important secret, but who refused to speak . . . He thought back to the groans coming from beneath the floor.

Mrs. Weatherspoon was obviously a part of whatever was happening, but what about Mr. Paulfrey? This sort of thing couldn't be going on at Mystery Mansion without him knowing about it. In fact, whatever was taking place in the cellar, Harry was willing to bet that the butler was something to do with it. He was such a cruel and evil man. Who could he and Anna turn to? They wouldn't dare speak to Lord Rakenhell, whose furious face glared down on them from so many portraits throughout the house.

The following night, Harry and Anna arranged to hide in the kitchen and watch the trap door. Hours passed, and nothing happened. There were no strange noises or visitors. Anna was almost dozing off, when she spotted a light through the kitchen window. Someone was moving inside the ruins of the chapel on the far end of the sloping lawn. She beckoned Harry over and they looked out into the night.

Three human figures were moving about between the crumbling walls and broken pillars. Each one of them held a lantern, the light from which glinted against the chapel's one remaining stained glass window.

"What shall we do now?" asked Anna.

"Go to the ruined chapel and investigate, of course," whispered Harry.

The chapel had been built at the same time as the house, but whereas Mystery Mansion had been built on rock, the chapel had been built on land that wasn't as firm as the builders had imagined. Within a hundred years, it had started to collapse.

The villagers had said that it was a sign from God. The then Lord Rakenhell had said it was the sign of a bad builder. The chapel had been left as a ruin and never repaired.

Harry and Anna stole across the moonlit lawn, carefully keeping to the shadows. Crouching behind the base of an enormous pillar, they spied on the figures before them. One was the man who had come out of the trap door the night before. The second was Mr. Paulfrey – so Harry had been right. But it was the sight of the third figure that really caused Harry to draw a sharp breath.

Hissing instructions through gritted teeth was someone both Harry and Anna had only ever seen in paintings. It was Lord Rakenhell himself. "Dig man! Dig!" he ordered, lighting an area of grass with his lantern. Mr. Paulfrey thrust the tip of his shovel into the marshy ground.

Harry had the feeling that he and Anna were uninvited guests at a burial.

Hound from Hell

Anna and Harry crouched as still as statues, watching the digging with gruesome fascination. What dark deed was Lord Rakenhell involved in? Whatever it was, no one was going to take a boot boy's word against the Lord of Mystery Mansion.

Harry watched in amazement as Mr. Paulfrey dug deep into the soil. What was happening? Neither he nor Anna had ever seen the butler getting his hands dirty before. He shuddered as the spade glinted in the moonlight.

Harry's thoughts were interrupted by a growl. It was a menacing growl that the boot boy and the dusting duty maid knew only too well – the growl of Lazarus, Lord Rakenhell's pet hound. This was a dog so big and so mean that no one, except Lord Rakenhell and Mr. Paulfrey, would go near him.

Before they knew it, Lazarus was launching his huge hairy body at them. Harry and Anna didn't stop to think. They didn't have time to worry about being seen. They fled.

"After them!" yelled Lord Rakenhell. His voice rang out like the crack of a whip in the darkness.

Harry and Anna ran for their lives. Harry could actually feel the warmth of Lazarus's breath at his ankles. The beast's snarling, slavering jaws only narrowly missed his flesh.

Breathless, and with pains in his side, Harry clambered over a low wall and kept on running. Anna was ahead of him now but, far more seriously, the hound was still behind him. Mist swirled out of nowhere, blotting out the moon. The darkness covered them like a shroud. "Where are you?" Anna cried out.

"Don't worry about me!" he shouted. "Just keep running." There was another snarl from Lazarus who was so close to Harry that Harry almost screamed in terror. This was a living nightmare.

In that instant, Harry felt the ground give way beneath his feet. They were on marshland . . . and he was sinking. Harry was about to shout a warning to Anna when Lazarus appeared out of the mist and gripped his arm between his snarling jaws. He didn't know which would be worse – drowning or being ripped to shreds . . .

A Helping Hand

Just as Harry thought his end had come, a horrid figure appeared, his head wrapped in bandages. Grabbing the dog by the collar, the awful stranger muttered a stern command. The dog released his vice-like grip on Harry's arm then, tail between his legs, trotted off into the night.

"Do exactly as I say and you shall be safe," said the stranger. Despite his terrifying appearance, Harry felt much calmer now the man was here. "You mustn't struggle. The more you wriggle, the quicker the ground will swallow you up."

Harry stayed absolutely still and grasped the man's hands. He found himself being pulled from the swamp like a cork being pulled from the neck of a bottle. Moments later, he found himself standing on the safety of solid ground.

"Thank you," gasped Harry.

The stranger thrust a filthy rag into his hand. "Hold this over your face," he ordered. "It's important not to breath in too much of this foul-smelling mist." A sudden surge of panic welled up inside Harry. He had been so pleased to be rescued that he'd forgotten Anna.

"Anna," he cried. "What about Anna?" The bandaged man grabbed Harry's wrist.

"Keep your voice down," he urged. "Do you want Lord Rakenhell to hear you? Don't go running off again, it's too dangerous. I know the safe paths through here, even by night, but you could perish without me to lead you." Harry frantically explained that he hadn't been alone. "I'll be back for her," began the man. Just then, a familiar voice wafted through the mist. It was the voice of Lord Rakenhell.

"Whoever they are, they must have stumbled into the marsh, poor devils," he said. "There's no hope for them now."

"Fools!" said Mr. Paulfrey. "Serves them right for prying into other people's affairs."

"Rather a harsh lesson," came the third voice, belonging to the man Harry had seen in the kitchen. The party turned and headed back to the chapel, where their task still awaited them. Harry shuddered and turned to face his rescuer.

"You must come with me," said the stranger with the bandaged face. "You must tread where I tread. Sidestep where I sidestep. One false move and you could end up sinking faster than I can pull you out. Ready?" Harry nodded. "Good," said the man. "And remember. Keep the cloth over your face."

Slowly, they began their treacherous journey across the marshland. Harry was worried about Anna, but tried hard to concentrate. Who was his strange rescuer? Did he really live out here in the wilds of the marsh? And what horrors lurked beneath those brown-stained bandages? The man had certainly saved his life, but to what end? Where were they going? Was he being led to a fate worse than being sucked into the depths of the earth? . . .

Then the wailing began. It seemed to be coming from everywhere. Harry peered through the mist and screamed in terror. He saw the boggy ground fill with skeletons, arms outstretched, moaning to be saved.

The Patient

Meanwhile, not far away, Magnus Duggan woke up with a groan. An aching in his head pounded like a blacksmith's hammer on an anvil. He tried to focus, but everything was a blur. A face came into view, but he didn't recognize the features.

"Hello, Mr. Duggan," said a woman. There was kindness in her voice. A cold sponge was wiped across his forehead. It felt refreshingly good. "How are you feeling today?"

Duggan struggled to say that he was feeling a little better, but couldn't form the words. They came out as meaningless grunts. The kind woman patted his arm. "Don't worry," she reassured him. "The words will come with time. You're in good hands here."

The clock winder wondered where 'here' was. He could remember falling down the stairs after seeing all those bats . . . the bats from his terrible nightmares. He could remember being taken back to his little cottage on the edge of the marsh, but the rest was a blank. The next thing he could recall was drifting in and out of sleep and waking up wherever he was now.

"W-W-Wuramee?" he said, after great effort. The blurred image of the woman's face came closer as she leaned over him to try to catch what he was saying.

"Wuramee?" he repeated.

"*Worry me*? Is that what you're trying to say? I'm sorry," said the woman. "I can't understand. The doctor will be here again soon."

Inside his head, Magnus Duggan was trying to ask '*Where am I?*' but it just wouldn't come out right. He felt so frustrated. The pounding in his head grew worse.

A square of light was carved out of the darkness above him. He could hear the rumble of voices followed by footsteps. The blurred image of the kind woman was replaced by that of a man.

"How is he?" he asked, lifting Duggan's right arm and taking his pulse.

"Much better. He's even trying to speak now, doctor," said the woman.

So this man is a doctor, thought Duggan. But this isn't a hospital. If only I could think straight.

Another person loomed into view. There was no mistaking who this was. "Are you still having nightmares, Mr. Duggan?" asked Lord Rakenhell with a smile.

A Place of Safety

When Harry opened his eyes, it was daytime and he was no longer trekking through the marsh. In fact, the first thing he saw was Anna, and she was very much alive and well. He was so pleased to see her.

"It's about time you woke up," she grinned. "You've been asleep for ages."
Harry looked around the strange room he was in. It was small, but bright and warm.

"Tell me it was all a dream," he said. "Mr. Paulfrey digging in the chapel at the dead of night . . . Lazurus chasing us . . . those skeletons all coming to life."

"You must have imagined the skeletons," Anna smiled. "But I'm afraid the rest certainly happened." She shuddered, remembering it all.

"You were lucky you didn't get sucked into the marsh," said Harry.

"I lost you in the mist . . . I couldn't see or hear you," Anna recalled. "Then something incredible happened. I thought I saw my dead mother. Her ghost led me along the only safe path . . . she saved me. Then Ralph found me and brought me here."

"Who's Ralph?" asked Harry.

"I am," said a tall and rather handsome man walking into the room. "We've already met, but I had my head wrapped in bandages. Remember?"

Harry remembered all right. This was the man who had saved him from the jaws of Lazarus and the damp grave of the marshland. "Thank you for saving my life, sir," he said.

"Forget the *sir*," smiled Ralph with a flash of brilliant white teeth. "You're not at Mystery Mansion now."

At the mention of Mystery Mansion, Harry's heart sank. Both he and Anna would have been reported missing. It wouldn't have taken Mr. Paulfrey long to put two and two together. The butler would soon realize that they were the ones who had been spying on the night-time activities by the chapel – that they were the ones who had been chased by Lazarus.

"At least they won't be searching for you two," said Ralph. He took a log from a basket and started a small fire in the grate. "Lord Rakenhell seemed to think you were both drowned in the marsh."

"But our duties – " began Anna.

"Do you mean to tell me you *want* to go back to work there?" asked Ralph in disbelief.

"We've nowhere else to go, sir," said Harry. He couldn't help calling his rescuer 'sir' because he was trained to address gentlemen in that manner. And Ralph was obviously a gentleman.

"I'm sorry," he said. "Of course not. It was a stupid thing to say."

There was something instantly likeable about Ralph, but what was he doing wandering around the marshes, his head wrapped in bandages? And how had he managed to control Lazarus? *Who* exactly was this man? And could he be trusted?

The Man Called Ralph

Ralph cooked Harry and Anna the biggest and best breakfast they'd ever eaten before. At Mystery Mansion, breakfast was usually a slice of bread with a smear of grease instead of butter. Ralph fried them bacon, sausages, eggs, fried bread . . . the menu seemed endless. It wasn't only the best breakfast Harry had ever had, it was the best *meal* he'd ever had in his whole life.

"That should put some meat on your bones," grinned Ralph, watching Harry eat the last morsel from his plate.

The mention of bones reminded Harry of the skeletons he had seen in the night. He shivered. They were as real to him as Anna and Ralph were now.

"Can I ask you a few questions Ralph?" he asked.

"Go ahead," said Ralph. "If I were in your shoes, there would be plenty of questions I'd be itching to ask."

Harry wasn't sure where to begin. "Why did you have bandages wrapped around your head when you rescued me last night?" he started.

His rescuer grinned. "Three reasons. One, to frighten people who might see me skulking about. Two, so that nobody will recognize me. And three, so that I don't breathe in all that horrible marsh gas."

"What's marsh gas?" asked Anna.

"It's the mist that you see hovering above the marshes," said Ralph. "Sometimes it even casts an eerie glow in the dark. It's a gas made by all the different chemicals in the rotting vegetation in the mud and water. It can be dangerous if you breathe in too much. That's why I made you both hold cloths over your faces."

"But why should you want to frighten people?" asked Harry. "You've been so kind to us." Ralph looked from Anna to Harry, then back again.

"There are many strange things happening in and around Mystery Mansion . . . and not just nightmares that seem to come true," he said. "Those who seem to be enemies could well be friends but, far more frighteningly, friends could turn out to be foe."

A silence fell around the table, only to be interrupted by Harry's tummy gurgling. All three of them burst out laughing. Harry turned bright red.

"But why don't you want people to recognize you, Ralph?" continued Anna. "Forgive me for asking, but have you done something wrong?"

Ralph laughed. "Well, to start with, I must confess that my real name isn't Ralph," he said. "I have good reasons for not wanting certain people to know I'm in these parts. I'm up against the Jack O'Lantern, and –"

"Who is Jack O'Lantern?" Harry interrupted. "Is he behind all the strange happenings around Mystery Mansion?"

"It's not a man we're up against, Harry," said the man who called himself Ralph. "If only Jack O'Lantern was really flesh and blood. No. He's no human being. He's far more dangerous than that . . ."

125

What Next?

Ralph wouldn't answer any more questions there and then. "There's work to be done," he said. Harry and Anna couldn't go back to work at Mystery Mansion but, at the same time, they couldn't stay with Ralph forever, either. There was the added problem that the few things they did own between them were still back at the house.

"That's easily solved," said Ralph. "I have a friend inside the household. He can gather together your belongings and leave them somewhere nearby for you to collect."

"Who is he?" asked Harry excitedly.

"That must remain a secret. He will not be told that you are both alive, and I won't reveal his identity. It's only fair."

Ralph explained that he usually stayed indoors until after dark, except when he had to attend to "matters of some urgency". Obviously, today he had a number of these to attend to because he went out that afternoon. He didn't wrap bandages around his head, but he did wrap a large scarf across the lower half of his face and pulled a large hat down to his eyes. Harry thought he was unrecognizable.

Left alone in the cottage, Anna and Harry began to realize just how upside down their lives had been turned. To go from being a maid and a boot boy, to stumbling on some extraordinary events and now be thought dead.

Harry wished he could make sense of all he had seen. The trap door in the kitchen. The digging in the chapel ruins. The man who called himself Ralph, and the Jack O'Lantern that was not a person but a *thing*.

And there was something vaguely familiar about their handsome host who had saved him from the jaws of Lazarus, and them both from a slow and awful death in the marsh . . . and he *had* seen those terrifying skeletons. He knew it. They had been so real. Harry wanted to find out more.

They decided to search the cottage for clues, although they did feel rather guilty at taking advantage of their host's hospitality. What kind of clues they were looking for, they weren't sure. Something to reveal his identity perhaps.

Harry had just entered a small study when there was a knock at the window. He looked up, and his jaw dropped in amazement.

At the other side of the leaded pane glass stood Miss Charlotte Rakenhell, like he had never seen her before. There was a look of complete and utter amazement on her face.

She raised a dainty white-gloved hand and pointed to him through the glass.

"You're dead!" she cried. "You . . . you thief. You're supposed to be dead!"

News from Mystery Mansion

Harry dashed to the front door of the cottage and steered the stunned Charlotte inside. She sat herself in an armchair. He had so much to tell her . . . about her father ordering Mr. Paulfrey to dig in the ruins of the chapel at the dead of night . . . about the skeletons . . . about Ralph and this cottage.

Harry frowned. "How did you know where to find us?" he asked.

"You must be Anna," said Charlotte, ignoring the question. "I was told you were both dead, but here you are, with Harry looking healthier and happier than I've ever seen him before. Extraordinary."

"Who said I was dead?" asked Harry. "And what did you mean by calling me a thief just then?"

Charlotte leaned forward and told Harry and Anna what had happened the night before . . .

128

"But that's a lie!" cried Anna . "We didn't steal anything."

"I'm no thief," said Harry indignantly. "That story must have been made up to hide the true facts and to explain our disappearance."

"Then you must come back with me to Mystery Mansion right this minute. We must tell my father of Paulfrey's lies," said Charlotte, leaping to her feet.

Harry took a deep breath. "It's not that simple, miss," he said nervously. "Mr. Paulfrey may be spreading those lies on your father's instructions!"

A Doctor Named Grimm

While Harry and Anna were listening to Charlotte's story of Mr. Paulfrey's lies, Magnus Duggan lay in a windowless room less than a mile away. He had to rely on the woman nursing him to tell him the time of day.

He soon gathered that the woman only came to sit with him at night. Now that the headaches had lessened and his vision had improved, she had introduced herself as Mrs. Weatherspoon, housekeeper of Mystery Mansion. This puzzled the clock winder. Why should Lord Rakenhell's housekeeper be caring for him?

Apart from the one visit from the Lord of Mystery Mansion and one or two from Mr. Paulfrey, the only other person Duggan had met was standing by his bed now.

"Didn't I say that I would have our patient talking in no time? How are you feeling, Mr. Duggan?" he asked.

"Much better, thank you. Are you by any chance the doctor?" asked the clock winder.

"Indeed I am, Mr. Duggan. I apologize for not having formally introduced myself," said the man. "My name is Roylott Grimm."

"Dr. Roylott Grimm? Lord Rakenhell's personal doctor!" said the patient with surprise. "But what are you doing caring for me, just a humble clock winder with a bump on my head?"

"There's been a great deal more wrong with you than that my good man," said the doctor. "What about your nightmares? What about the vampire bats?"

130

In the flickering candle light, the doctor's eyes gleamed. Standing half in shadow, his cloak made him look strangely bat-like himself.

Magnus Duggan tried to sit up, but the effort was too great for him, and he rested his head back down on the pillow. "They were just dreams – nightmares – as you yourself said, sir."

Dr. Roylott Grimm rummaged around in his black bag. "Those who suffer nightmares on the estate of Mystery Mansion do not suffer *ordinary* nightmares, Mr. Duggan," he said. "More often than not, their nightmares eventually appear to come true."

Dr. Grimm produced a large syringe full of blue liquid and advanced toward the bed. "This is for your own good. Trust me," he smiled.

Duggan felt the prick in his arm, and immediately began to feel sleepy . . . sleepy . . . sleepy . . . His head began to spin and all he could focus on was Dr. Roylott Grimm's face – the words 'Jack O'Lantern', echoing inside his head.

Living Nightmares

Thora Mulch, the village gossip, had never been more than a few miles from the village in her entire life. She had been born in the village, been to school in the village and married in the village. She knew every building, every tree and every corner of every street. She knew everybody and everybody's business.

She was proud of her reputation as the local gossip. The old woman made a career of it, even more so since her husband had died a few years back. But until now, she hadn't actually *believed* much of what she said about the strange happenings at Mystery Mansion.

But now Thora had been having terrible nightmares. Nightmares that her dear departed husband, Norman had come back from the dead. He had died one night when he tripped over their cat, Jago, and broke his neck. The nightmare always began with the yowl of the cat and then Norman came toward her, his neck strangely twisted and his head lolling forward on his chest. It all seemed so real. Thora was very frightened.

Thora Mulch didn't tell anyone of the dream that haunted her night after night. She was beginning to be afraid to go out – except, of course, for her trips to *The Bogside Inn*. Hadn't Magnus Duggan's dreams of bats come true, and now he'd disappeared? What might happen to her?

Then Thora began to think back to other villagers in the past. Old Ma Gibbon who had thrown herself under a cart screaming that the witch hunters were after her. Thomas Bridmore who had disappeared from the village claiming that every night the shadows on his walls cried out to him. Thora shuddered and pulled her shawl tighter around her. Would she be next?

Outside, the wind was blowing, blanketing the village in mist. But Jago needed feeding so Thora had to go out. She sighed and stepped outside, setting off in the direction of the butcher. There was no one else around. Then she thought she heard footsteps – slow, deliberate footsteps somewhere behind her. But when she stopped, the footsteps stopped, so she started off again . . . as did the footsteps behind her. "Who's there?" she demanded, peering through the mist.

Thora could just make out a shadowy form with a strangely twisted neck and lolling head. She screamed, collapsing to the ground in a crumpled heap.

Full Circle

I can't believe what you're saying Harry.

Back at the cottage, Charlotte Rakenhell's mind was reeling. "Are you trying to tell me that my father is behind some . . . some dreadful plot?" she spluttered.

"I hate to be disrespectful," said Anna. "But it does seem likely. I mean, Mr. Paulfrey does work for his lordship –"

"But as I've said to Harry before, Paulfrey is such a horrid man," said Charlotte, throwing open the front door and stepping outside. "He could be up to no good right under my father's nose."

Pulling on their warm clothes, Harry and Anna caught up with Charlotte. They came to the edge of the wood, and there was the river in front of them, with a fallen tree stretching across it like a bridge, and a hollow oak tree off to the left. It was there that Harry had been supposed to leave the package for Mr. Colly.

"This is where I rescued you!" he cried. Charlotte nodded.

"Rescue? What rescue?" asked Anna, looking from Harry to Charlotte and back again.

"Never mind," said Charlotte.

"You still haven't told us how you found us, Miss Charlotte," said Harry, looking around him. He had been brought to the cottage when unconscious, and Anna had been led there in the dark. Neither of them knew where they were.

"It was quite by chance," confessed Charlotte. "I was so upset by the news that you'd been sucked up by the marsh that . . ." she paused and turned away. "I wanted to be alone. I'd no idea that the old woodcutter's cottage was being lived in. It's been empty for years. I passed it quite by chance, and there you both were sitting inside. Alive and well."

"So you've no idea who the man who calls himself Ralph is, Miss Charlotte?" said Anna. "He's been very good to us. He saved our lives –"

"And gave us breakfast," Harry added.

Charlotte shook her head. "I doubt Father knows he's there either. I haven't heard any talk of a new tenant. Very strange. I wonder what this Ralph of yours is up to."

"Hey!" cried Harry. "I've just had a thought. Ralph said that he had a friend back at Mystery Mansion who could get us our belongings. That might be Mr. Colly, the head gardener. He gave me a package once and told me to put it in that tree over there." He pointed to the hollow oak. "Perhaps it was for Ralph, as his cottage is so close by."

"Why don't we ask him?" suggested Anna. "Here he comes now."

Sure enough, Ralph's figure had appeared, skirting the edge of the woodland. His hat was pulled low and his face was still covered by a scarf. What horrified the three children, however, was what he was carrying. It appeared to be the lifeless form of a woman.

A Face from the Past

Hurrying back to the cottage, Harry threw open the front door and stood aside to let Ralph past. Ralph gently laid the woman in an armchair. "You'll find some smelling salts in that cupboard, Harry," said Ralph. "Could you get them for me?"

"Who is she?" asked Anna.

Ralph moved the woman to a sitting position. "Her name is Thora Mulch," he said. "I gave her a fright when I came out of the mist. She seemed to think that I was someone named Norman."

On hearing the name, Thora Mulch opened an eye and moaned: "Norman? Is that you? Have you come back for me?"

Ralph wafted the smelling salts under her nose. "You're safe here, Mrs. Mulch. You're with friends."

When the smelling salts had worked their magic, Charlotte stepped forward from behind the chair. "I think that you owe us an explanation, sir," she said to Ralph. "And you could start by telling us your real name and what you are doing on my father's estate."

Ralph grinned and stood up. "I don't have to ask who *you* are," he chuckled. "I know I have the pleasure of addressing Miss Charlotte Lydia Rakenhell."

"Then you have me at an advantage, sir," said Charlotte.

Ralph roared with laughter, which seemed to upset Mrs. Mulch. He patted her hand and whispered soothing words.

"My identity can wait," he said. "Anna, please will you make Mrs. Mulch some tea. You'll find some in the kitchen."

Anna went out to the hand pump outside the back door to draw some water for the tea. She had just begun to lower the handle when she heard a loud growl. It was the deep, throaty snarl of Lazarus. The maid froze in fear.

"Oh, look who's here," said a cruel voice. "So little Anna isn't dead at all, but hiding out in the woods."

Anna turned to face Mr. Paulfrey, who was having trouble holding Lazarus on his leash. The steam from the dog's slavering jaws rose into the cold air like smoke from a dragon's mouth.

"I –I–I can explain . . ." Anna whimpered, terrified by the sight of the dog.

"Explain?" said Mr. Paulfrey. "What is there to explain? If everyone already thinks you're dead, then why disappoint them?" He bent down and unclasped Lazarus's collar from the leash. "Kill!" he screamed, a crazed laugh rising in his throat.

The Rage

Meanwhile, in the library at Mystery Mansion, Lord Rackenhell was in a rage. He hurled a glass across the room and it shattered into a thousand shards. "Are you telling me you don't know where my daughter is?" he bellowed.

Mrs. Weatherspoon, the victim of his lordship's rage, did not flinch. "Mr. Paulfrey is looking for Miss Charlotte now, your lordship," she reassured him. "There is no cause for alarm."

Rakenhell snorted like a wounded bull elephant. "*No cause for alarm*, you say? I have a son and heir who has deserted me. I have a house and estate built on this godforsaken marsh, and idiots like you and Paulfrey for servants . . . and you say that there is no cause for alarm. I want my daughter. *Now!*"

Mrs. Weatherspoon scowled and put her hands on her hips. "Your lordship – Henry – in the past you have asked me to tell you if and when you start behaving like a spoiled child. Well, I have to tell you. You are behaving like a spoiled child right now."

Lord Rakenhell went the brightest shade of purple the housekeeper had ever seen. *"What did you say?"* he screamed. "You should be taken from this place and horsewhipped woman."

Mrs. Weatherspoon continued to scowl. "If that isn't further proof that your lordship is behaving like a spoiled child, I don't know what is. If that will be all, I have other duties."

To her utter amazement, Rakenhell threw himself to the ground and began to pummel the polished wooden floor with his fists. "I am your lord and master!" he yelled. "My word is law!" Somehow, he became entangled in a tiger skin rug and appeared to be wrestling with a live creature. "Get this thing off me!" he howled. "Get it off."

At that moment, Dr. Roylott Grimm entered the library. He had heard the commotion from the hallway and was already brandishing a syringe when he entered the room. "Calm yourself, Henry! Calm yourself!" he urged.

Mrs. Weatherspoon sat on Lord Rakenhell to keep him still while Dr. Grimm administered the injection into his arm. The tiger skin lay lifeless on the floor. "We're going to have to get his lordship and Miss Charlotte away from here," said the housekeeper. "He can't take much more of this."

"None of us can, Mrs. Weatherspoon," said the doctor, feeling the pulse of Lord Rakenhell who was now drifting off into sleep. "Jack O'Lantern is working his evil into all of us. He could ruin us all yet. He could ruin us all."

The Master

A split second before Lazarus launched himself on top of the terrified Anna, a voice rang out through the woods like a gun shot. "No boy!" cried Ralph, and the hound slumped to the ground with ears flat, whimpering like a harmless puppy.

It was hard to tell who was more stunned, Anna or Mr. Paulfrey. Both of them were shaking – Mr. Paulfrey with anger and Anna with fear, which was now turning to relief. Harry and Charlotte tumbled out of the back door to see what all the commotion was about.

"Paulfrey, what are you doing here?" demanded the young Miss Rakenhell.

"Looking for you Miss," explained the butler. "It seems I've uncovered a whole hornets' nest. I don't think your father will be too pleased to hear that you have been mixing with thieving servants . . . and whoever this may be." His gaze locked on to Ralph's face. "I feel sure *we*'ve met before," he said.

"Of course we have, Paulfrey," sneered Ralph, with a coldness in his voice the children had not heard before. "I wouldn't expect Charlotte to remember me too clearly. She was so young when I went away. But you, Paulfrey? Look at this face. Older, perhaps, but have I really changed that much?"

The butler's jaw dropped. "It's . . . you're . . ."

Ralph whistled through his teeth and Lazarus bounded over to him. "Yes Paulfrey. I'm Edmund Rakenhell, who you were so cruel to as a boy. My father was too busy battling Jack O'Lantern to listen to me. Perhaps he'll listen now."

It was Charlotte's turn to be stunned. Ralph was none other than her long lost brother, heir to Mystery Mansion and nothing but a dim memory until now. "Edmund!" she whooped with delight, throwing herself at him.

"Welcome back, Master Edmund," said Mr. Paulfrey, with a sneer. "I'm afraid you'll find your poor father still the same as ever . . . only more so. Quite off his head in fact." He laughed.

"Tell me something I don't already know, Paulfrey. I'm here to put a stop to all this madness. My father's madness, his rages and all the unspeakable nightmares that have gripped the villagers for far too long," said Edmund.

"I somehow doubt that," said Mr. Paulfrey.

"My father, Dr. Grimm, Mrs. Weatherspoon and all the others have been trying to do some good but what they didn't realize was that *you* have been turning everything to your own advantage," said Edmund. "You don't want my father to be cured or clear-headed. You want Jack O'Lantern to get him like the rest of them. But you've failed, Paulfrey. You've failed."

"Don't think you've beaten me yet – any of you!" Paulfrey cried. He turned and ran, leaving a trail of terrifying laughter behind him. It was the laughter of a madman.

Back at Mystery Mansion

Harry and Anna returned to Mystery Mansion in style. They went through the main entrance and into the drawing room with Edmund and Charlotte. Here, Lord Rakenhell was resting on a couch, flanked by Mrs. Weatherspoon and Dr. Roylott Grimm. Mrs. Weatherspoon recognized Edmund Rakenhell at once, and there was much weeping and hugging all around.

When the excitement of reunion was over, attention turned to Harry and Anna who looked out of place in all this grandeur. "And who are these two?" asked Lord Rakenhell, quietly.

"The two servants you thought had perished in the marshland when chased by Lazarus, father," said Edmund.

"The thieves!" said his lordship, struggling to sit up. "But at least you're alive. No one deserves to die in that marsh."

"Not thieves, but innocent children who stumbled on your secrets beneath the kitchen and your digging by the ruined chapel, father. I've no doubt Paulfrey took advantage of the situation and stole some of the silver for himself. He's been cheating you for years," said Edmund. "We owe Harry and Anna here an explanation."

Lord Rakenhell sighed. "And I trusted him. I am at the end of my tether. After generations, I think that the Rakenhells should admit defeat and leave Mystery Mansion. Let nature and Jack O'Lantern reclaim this terrible part of the country."

"I don't understand," protested Anna. "How can this Jack O'Lantern have the Rakenhells on the run?"

"Jack O'Lantern is just one of its names. Another is will-o'-the-wisp or *ignis fatuus*," explained Dr. Grimm. "It's the pale glow you sometimes see over the marshland around Mystery Mansion at night. It's caused by the mixture of gases created by decomposing organic matter – "

Harry and Anna looked at him blankly. "What the doctor means, is that the rotting plants in the marshland mix together to form strange marsh gases," said Edmund Rakenhell. "It's these gases which gave this house the name *Misty Mansion*. And that give people nightmares and make them see things."

"You have to breathe a lot of the marsh gas over many years for it to affect the mind badly," the doctor reassured them. "Mr. Duggan, who we are caring for in the hideaway under the kitchen, has lived in the village for fifty years and it has only recently started to muddle his brain and make him see imaginary bats. Not one of us in this room has been seriously affected . . . except his lordship –"

"Who has made it his life to try to find a way to beat the marsh gas, without letting on to outsiders that it is anything more than a bad-smelling mist," Edmund Rakenhell interrupted. "Hence hiding away and caring for the sick, and taking soil samples from the chapel. Sadly, Jack O'Lantern has given you rages, father, and let Paulfrey trick you at every turn."

"But what made you come back?" Harry asked.

"I haven't wasted my years away from Mystery Mansion. I've come back to stay. We all can. I'm a man of science and have spent my time researching the problem," said Edmund proudly. "By growing certain new plants in the marshland, we'll be able to produce a new gas – one which makes all the other gases harmless. The nightmares will be over for everyone. Once and for all."

Did You Spot?

You can use this page to help spot things that could be useful in solving the mystery. First, there are hints and clues you can read as you go along. They will give you some idea of what to look out for. Then there are extra notes to read which tell you more about what happened afterwards.

Hints and Clues

99	The grave digger's nightmare appears to have come true.
100-101	The parcel could be an important clue to someone's identity later.
104-105	What could have happened to the package?
106-107	Hmm. Another example of nightmares coming to life?
108-109	There can be more than just a supernatural explanation for the blank wall.
110-111	Plenty of big, old houses have cellars.
112-113	Mystery, Misty, Misery or Miserly. What's in a name?
114-115	The soil itself might be important.
118-119	Lazarus was quick to obey the bandaged stranger. Could he know him?
120-121	Is that a *square* of light in the roof above Duggan? Where could he be being held?
122-123	Surely it's a little strange to have a picture of a plant in a photo frame?
124-125	Lanterns give off light.
126-127	Study the items in the room with care.
130-131	Ah. So could it be that Magnus Duggan is being kept in the cellar?
132-133	The figure in the mist looks familiar.
134-135	You should know who Ralph is carrying.
136-137	How could Ralph know Charlotte?
138-139	From the way Mrs. Weatherspoon has been talking, his lordship sounds ill.
140-141	Everything should begin to fall into place from now on.

In the End

Edmund Rakenhell's plan to make the marsh gases around Mystery Mansion harmless worked. Today, there are still mists in the village and near the house, but they neither glow in the dark, nor make people see things.

Magnus Duggan and Thora Mulch both made full recoveries.

Life at Mystery Mansion changed for everyone after Edmund's return. On Dr. Grimm's orders, Lord Rakenhell went to Europe to get better. Edmund took over the running of the house and the servants became some of the best-treated for miles around.

When Harry grew up, he became a butler. Miss Charlotte married a man called Lord Snortle and had seven children.

Inspired by Edmund's example, Anna became fascinated by plants. With help from the Rakenhell family, she was awarded a university scholarship. She later became one of the world's leading experts on plant life.

The body of Mr. Paulfrey was found floating in the marshland near Mystery Mansion. Jack O'Lantern had claimed one last victim.

By the way . . .

The doorway behind the tapestry (on page 13) was bricked up by Mr. Paulfrey. He had filled the storage cupboard with his ill-gotten gains. Over the years, he stole a great deal from the house.

Did you spot the items in the room on page 31? – a microscope on the table to help Edmund with his experiments and a picture on the wall of him as a child with Lord Rakenhell.

First published in 1995 by Usborne Publishing Ltd, Usborne House, 83-85 Saffron Hill, London EC1N 8RT, England. Copyright © 1995 Usborne Publishing Ltd.

The name Usborne and the device are Trade Marks of Usborne Publishing Ltd.

Printed in Great Britain U.E.

First published in America March 1996